D1284469

Sea of Cortez

Garry Ryan

SEA OF CORTEZ

A Detective Lane Mystery

A NeWest
MYSTERY

COPYRIGHT © GARRY RYAN 2018

LIBRARY AND ARCHIVES CANADA CATALOGUING IN PUBLICATION

Ryan, Garry, 1953–, author
Sea of Cortez / Garry Ryan.

(Detective Lane mystery ; 10) Issued in print and electronic formats.
ISBN 978-1-988732-39-8 (softcover).
ISBN 978-1-988732-40-4 (epub).
ISBN 978-1-988732-41-1 (Kindle)

I. Title.   II. Series: Ryan, Garry, 1953– . Detective Lane mystery ; 10.

PS8635.Y354S43 2018   C813'.6   C2018-900601-3   C2018-900602-1

Editor for the Board: Leslie Vermeer
Cover and interior design: Natalie Olsen, Kisscut Design
Front cover photo: Garry Ryan   **Back cover photo:** Kevin Tadge / Stocksy.com
Interior photo (page 1): Pixel Stories / Stocksy.com
Author photo: Luke Towers

NeWest Press acknowledges the support of the Canada Council for the Arts, the Alberta Foundation for the Arts, and the Edmonton Arts Council for support of our publishing program. We acknowledge the financial support of the Government of Canada through the Canada Book Fund for our publishing activities.

NeWest Press wishes to acknowledge that the land on which we operate is Treaty 6 territory and a traditional meeting ground and home for many Indigenous Peoples, including Cree, Saulteaux, Niisitapi (Blackfoot), Métis, and Nakota Sioux.

#201, 8540–109 Street
Edmonton, Alberta T6G 1E6
780.432.9427
www.newestpress.com

No bison were harmed in the making of this book.
Printed and bound in Canada

for
Karma,
Ben
and
Luke

chapter 1

Lane looked at orange gold schooling beyond the toes of his black and red cross trainers. The kokanee rested before attempting another swim against the current and up through the culvert. The pipe was a metre in diameter and ran perpendicular to the two-lane paved road that had carried Lane and Arthur here. The highway was about thirty metres above the stream it bisected. Lane watched an exhausted fish being swept back out of the pipe and into the stream. The water's usual olive green was visible here and there as it flowed downstream and into Lake Koocanusa. The lake was one hundred forty-five kilometres long and shared by BC and Montana. It ran roughly north and south along a valley in the Kootenay Rockies. Arthur had turned off the paved road on the east side of the lake along the way to a place called Jaffray.

It was a dusty ten degrees Celsius in a valley predominantly forested with evergreens. Lane watched the wavering gold under the rippling surface. *These fish don't know or care which side of the border they are on.* He looked west toward the lake, but all he could see was some of the creek's white water, trees and the thick undergrowth.

Arthur, Lane's partner, put his hand on Lane's shoulder. "My dad brought us here when I was eight or nine. He said Canadians didn't appreciate what is right under their noses. He called the spawning of the kokanee one of God's great miracles. They are born together, they die together and they give life to the next generation." Arthur lifted his Blue Jays ball cap and wiped sweat off his scalp with the sleeve of his shirt. "I was more interested in the rocks." He bent to pick up a grey stone shaped like a boomerang. Arthur's round Mediterranean face was lit with a smile. "See what I mean?"

Lane smiled and looked back to the gentler waters between the culvert and the rapids downstream. Thousands of kokanee waited their turn in the relatively calmer waters. *I have never seen anything quite like this. What makes them gather together for generation after generation to swim upstream to spawn and die?*

"You gotta watch out for the bears." A man stepped out of the trailer parked about ten metres back from the stream. He wore a frayed, grey-faded green shirt, grey–green work pants belted with a rope and lace-free white running shoes. The man's black hair was uncombed. His face and hands told the story of twenty or thirty years of outdoor labour.

Lane smiled and pulled up the waist of his black pants. *These things must be stretching.* "Any around today?"

"Not so far but they will come. Always do." The man lit a cigarette with an orange plastic lighter and inhaled a lungful. He pulled the cigarette out with his right hand and used it to point at Lane and Arthur. "You guys are from?"

Lane lifted his chin. "Calgary. And you?"

"Just up the road. Jaffray. Needed to get away from people for a few days. The kokanee are late, the snow is late and everyone is arguin' about climate change." The man turned, walked downstream and disappeared behind the trailer.

Arthur frowned at Lane. "Scary-looking fellow."

"Gave us some friendly advice, though." Lane looked back at the stream where the fish turned the water from green to a shifting, shimmering red gold. *Lots of food just waiting for a hungry bear.*

"What's that?" Arthur pointed downstream where the fish had to fight the white water to reach the pool below the culvert. A black bear perched on the edge of the far bank, then waded into the stream and climbed up onto a rock where it began to scoop with the open claws of its right paw.

"Maybe we'd better go back to the car." Lane reached out and tugged the back of Arthur's white nylon shirt. The bear continued to fish as they watched it balance on three paws atop a flat rock. *The bear is solitary, a hunter. The kokanee gather in a school.*

When they got into the car Arthur said, "We probably could have stayed and watched. The bear was totally ignoring us."

The man from the trailer reappeared and zipped up his fly as he puffed on the cigarette. He walked over to the BMW. Arthur opened his window. The man said, "If you drive up the road about six miles you'll find Little Sand Creek. There'll be more fish there." He turned and pointed at the busy black bear. "That black bear probably won't bother you, but there's been a grizzly around this week and he's kind of ornery." The man gave them a tip of an imaginary hat and waved as he walked back to his trailer.

Lane drove up the trail. It wound its way up to the two-lane highway. They headed north on the pavement lined with evergreen trees. The sun shone through Lane's window. He checked the odometer and made some mental calculations. "Six miles. That's about ten kilometres?"

Arthur looked out his window. "Dr. Keller said a holiday this winter would do us both good. He suggested some sunshine and a beach."

Lane started to answer and closed his mouth. He reached to turn on the music. Arthur put his hand out to cover the radio's controls. "We're going to talk."

"About what?" Lane heard the defensiveness in his reply and shook his head. He looked in the mirror and saw panic in his blue eyes alongside the increasing grey in his once-black hair and the deepening creases across his forehead and at the corners of his eyes.

"About Christine, Dan and Indiana moving out. About what's been bothering you for months. About your weight loss. About all of it." Arthur looked out his window.

Lane inhaled a long, slow, exhausted breath.

"Dr. Keller says the weight loss is a symptom."

Lane eased into the curve and accelerated.

"Slow down! You're not going to avoid this conversation by scaring the shit out of me!"

Lane's right foot lifted off of the accelerator. "You drive, then!" He jammed on the brakes, pulled onto the shoulder and skidded to a halt in a dramatic cloud of dust.

Arthur put his hand on the dash and looked left at Lane. His eyes were round and wide, yet he kept his voice level. "I'm not going to talk clichés about what happened. You've heard them all and none of them have made it any easier."

Lane shoved the transmission into park, heaved on the emergency brake, got out of the car and slammed the door. He looked back along the road, then turned and looked ahead. No traffic either way. He heard Arthur's door open and his partner's footsteps crunching the gravel. Arthur stopped. Lane turned. His chest ached, and he realized he hadn't taken a breath. He inhaled, deeply, then took another breath. *Keep breathing. In and out. It will make it possible to think.*

Arthur crossed his arms and leaned against the back hatch.

Lane's anger began to cool. *Why not tell him? You never told anyone about what Lola said.* "Back in July Lola came to see me at the office. It was early. She pushed her way in and closed the door. She said that she and John had decided it would be better if her grandson were raised outside of a house where a killer lived. That it was nothing personal, that

I was only doing my job. But they were going to offer one of their properties to Dan and Christine rent free."

Arthur leaned forward, his feet shoulder width apart. "That odorous misandrist."

What? "I've never heard you say something like that before."

"I'm working on my vocabulary skills. Besides, Lola is an insult to my mother tongue. Why didn't you say anything to me or to Christine? You always think you have to carry this kind of thing on your own. I thought it was the shooting eating away at you."

"I knew she and Dan wanted a place of their own and if I told her what happened, well —" He held out his hands. "You know what would have happened."

"Christine would have told Lola to shove it."

Lane nodded.

"We all know what Lola's like, and most of us can tune her out." Arthur mimed turning a radio's knob. "Why'd she get under your skin and why keep it from us for so long? We've all been wondering what was eating at you."

"Because it was so easy for me." Lane stared at the pavement as a pickup whistled past. It left the stink of spent diesel fuel in the air.

"What was easy?"

"Killing. It was easy to kill Pierce. Just pull the trigger. I was surprised how effortless it was. I always thought that if I found myself in a situation like that, I'd find a way out other than killing. That's not what happened. I even thought about shooting Cori Pierce when I had her out there alone in the storm. So I was afraid Lola was right about me. That the killing made me different."

"But you didn't kill Cori Pierce. She's in jail now and not getting out. She and her husband can't hurt anyone else because you did what you had to."

Lane shook his head and shrugged. He looked at his feet,

expecting to see a pool of vomit with a red pepper or two from the morning's omelette he'd picked at. Or at the very least to feel a sense of relief as evidence of the release of the festering truth he'd just expelled. Enough time had passed; he wanted to move on, get over shooting Pierce, who would have felt no remorse at killing children. He lifted his head, inhaled and listened to the silence.

"You actually thought that Lola had a point? That Indiana would be better not living with us? Without *you*? That's why you've been putting distance between yourself and Christine and Dan and Indiana?"

Lane shrugged. *Why do I always feel that I'm about to be betrayed by those closest to me?*

Arthur shook his head and walked to the driver's door. "Get in." He waited until Lane was belted in, then asked, "Remember Lola's licence plate?"

"LOLAGETS?"

"Yes. Gets under your skin. She saw a scar and she scratched it open. People like her have a knack for spotting old wounds and weaknesses. She finds them and tears off the scab. The end justifies the means with her." Arthur shifted into drive, shoulder checked and stomped the accelerator. "She also has a talent for underestimating. She doesn't know what a ruthless bitch I can be."

Lane reached for the controls at the side of his seat. An electric motor whirred as his seat leaned back. For a while he watched the trees go by; then he closed his eyes, inhaling the scents of pine and spruce.

He woke up two hours later. He turned to look out the window and saw a man with shoulder-length red hair and a red beard. The man wore a conical black cap with silver stars and a cloak of red satin. Lane estimated the distance from the tip of his cap to the tip of his beard was at least a metre. "Where the hell are we?"

"Radium. Hungry? I checked at the gas station. There's all-you-can-eat ribs tonight at the diner. They're supposed to be pretty good. Want to try some after we get checked in?"

Lane turned to watch the wizard walk toward a ramshackle collection of buildings, wooden walls, totem poles and chainsaw sculptures. Lane's phone chirped. He pulled it out of his shirt pocket. The message was from Nigel. "Mexico. The Playa del Carmen police say Sean Pike has died from gunshot wounds." Lane pocketed the phone and stared ahead as they climbed the side of a mountain to a red-cedar-sided three-storey chalet at the end of the winding paved road.

An hour later Lane and Arthur sat across from each other at a booth inside Jacks. The restaurant was on a side street running parallel to the highway at the east side of Radium. The interior was done in wood: pine benches, spruce table tops, fir flooring, cedar support beams, knotty pine walls and chipboard ceiling. *Someone must have a connection at the local sawmill.* The parents across from them kept a pair of toddlers busy colouring on the brown paper covering their table. The little girl peeled the paper from her red crayon and licked it. The boy focused on the paper, held three crayons in one hand and drew an arc from left to right. "A rainbow!" his mother said.

"What was the text about?" Arthur asked.

Here comes dinner. Lane spotted the waitress wearing a white Coldplay T-shirt heading their way. She balanced two plates the size of platters. "Watch out boys, the plates are hot." She slid them onto the table and waltzed away. PINK was written in white across her tight-against-the-booty sweats.

Lane regarded the side of pork ribs basted with pepper sauce and accompanied by coleslaw and beans. "This is enough food for four or five people." He leaned forward and sniffed. *And it smells great!* He picked up the tail at the end of the ribs and took a bite. "Mmmmm!"

"You've got your appetite back." Arthur arranged wipes and napkins at his right-hand side, then in the middle of the table, before sawing three ribs off and getting started.

Lane sat back after finishing his second plate of ribs. He reached out and held his water glass with sticky fingers. Arthur's head was turned sideways; he watched Lane out of one eye with a smile on his lips. The boy at the next table studied the detective and frowned. "Daddy, he ate two plates!"

Lane looked at the boy. He felt the sauce drying on his lips and cheeks. There was laughter from another table. Then Arthur began to roar and most of the people in the restaurant joined in. Except, of course, for the little boy, whose eyes filled with tears. He leaned into his father, who put an arm around the child.

The waitress hustled over, looked down at Lane and lifted his plate. It was piled with napkins and bones. "Want some more ribs?"

Lane smiled and shook his head. "No, thanks, but I would like to buy ice cream for the little guys." He nodded his head toward the next table.

The waitress smiled. "Want me to ask?"

"Please."

A few moments passed in relative silence. Lane reached over and grabbed the wipes inside the plastic wrappers. His hands slipped over the shiny surface. He gripped the top of the black packet, but his fingers couldn't tear the packet open. "These things are impossible."

"What did the text say?" Arthur deftly tore open a pack and handed it to Lane.

Lane wiped his face and fingers. "That Sean Pike is dead from gunshot wounds in Playa del Carmen."

"Mexico?" Arthur leaned forward, picked up another packet, tore it open and handed the wipe across the table.

"Yes." Lane felt refreshing wetness on his face.

Arthur leaned back and laughed.

"What?"

"How much do you want to bet the body is already cremated?"

Lane shrugged. "We'll see."

"What happened to your ear?" a voice asked.

They looked over at the little boy, who had chocolate ice cream on his nose and cheeks and down the front of his shirt. He stood at the end of their table. His mother said, "You're supposed to say thank you for the ice cream, Isaac."

Lane smiled and reached for his missing earlobe. "No worries. I hope you liked the ice cream."

The boy smiled, turned and climbed back up onto his chair.

Arthur touched Lane's hand. "You think Lola would have the compassion to do what you did for that little one?" He rolled his eyes and shook his head. "You really need to learn how to listen to the people who are worth listening to and delete the rest."

chapter 2

They finished the ear-popping descent into the mountain valley of Kootenay National Park. Highway 93 levelled out and the trees on either side of the highway leaned in close. To the west, the trees climbed the side of a mountain range. To the east, the trees thinned in the rocky soil, providing brief glimpses of the Kootenay River.

Lane smiled and looked at his phone. The parkway was a dead zone as far as phones were concerned. Norah Jones, Corinne Bailey Rae, Jenn Grant, Bruce Springsteen and Hannah Georgas sang instead. He set the cruise at ninety-five kilometres per hour and settled into the seat. The road ahead was free of traffic. He glanced in the rear-view mirror. Three black wolves loped across the highway in single file as they headed for the river, their tails and noses forming one straight line. The trio of black ghosts disappeared into the trees one by one. The entire event took less than two seconds.

×

"See anything on your trip?" Matt finished off a slice of meat lover's pizza. He was letting his strawberry blond hair grow long and it now covered the tops of his ears. *I wonder if he'll ever gain any weight*, Lane thought as Matt got up from the table, hip-hop-skipped to the fridge and grabbed a jug of orange juice. He twisted off the cap, went to put it to his lips, caught a disapproving glance from his Uncle Arthur and instead grabbed a tumbler and sat down to pour the juice.

"I saw three wolves this morning." Lane poured himself some orange juice and offered the container to Arthur, who shook his head.

"You didn't tell me that," Arthur said.

Lane shrugged. "It lasted all of two seconds in the rear-view mirror."

Matt smiled, picked up another slice of pizza and pointed it at Lane. "So the big-city hunter saw some of his relatives. I'm surprised you didn't stop and follow them to share some tracking tips."

"Them and the bear," Arthur said.

"You saw a bear?" Matt chewed the end off the triangle of pizza.

"It was a black bear fishing for kokanee. Didn't take any notice of us." Arthur looked at the pizza box, reached for it then pulled his hand away.

"And we saw a wizard." Lane sipped his orange juice. *I wonder what Indiana is up to?*

Matt leaned back in his chair and lifted one eyebrow with frank skepticism. "Where?"

"Radium. Same place he—" Arthur pointed at his partner "—ate two plates of ribs."

"Mister fruits and vegetables ate two plates of ribs?" Matt covered his mouth and opened his eyes wide to complete the effect.

Lane shrugged. "It was kind of a disconnected, one-surprise-after-another trip."

Matt rolled his eyes. "You find connections in the most obscure places. Won't be long before you're telling us how it was all part of a bigger picture. You know, the hunter, the spawning kokanee and the magic that brings them all together."

✕

The phone rang. Matt pressed pause on his game controller and picked up the phone sitting beside him on the ottoman. "What's up?"

"What are you doing?" Christine asked.

"Watching TV."

"Which video game is it?"

"It's a car race. What do you want?" Matt restarted the game.

"They get home okay?"

"Yep." Matt leaned into the turn as his Porsche skidded around a hairpin.

"Was it a good trip?"

The Porsche fishtailed, exited the turn and accelerated onto a straightaway. "They saw kokanee, wolves, a bear and a wizard."

"They went to see beer?"

"The fish, not the beer. Kokanee the fish were spawning."

"Oh, sounds exciting."

"How's Indy doing?"

"He's sleeping, finally."

"Rough day?"

"He's getting new teeth."

"Sorry." Matt downshifted near the end of the straightaway. The Porsche skidded off the end of the track and bounced off the barrier. "Want to talk with Uncle Lane?"

"I don't think he wants to talk with me." Christine hung up.

×

Frederick waited in a car parked outside the Sleeping Dragon restaurant. He was seventeen. An hour ago, he'd slipped out of his parents' three-thousand-square-foot two-storey home with its three-car garage. His bedroom was beneath theirs and he could hear them fucking. Flesh slapping against flesh. Headboard smacking the wall. It reminded Frederick of their mantra: *A better life for the boy. A better life for the boy. A better life for the boy.* The code inherited from his grandmother, who'd come to this country when she was twenty-five to find a better life for *her* son. The grandmother who raised him while his parents worked. Gran, who loved him, pampered him, then deserted him at fourteen when she died from a three-pack-a-day heart attack.

He thought of these things as he leaned back in the leather seat of a black Infiniti with tinted windows and a sunroof. The front door of the Sleeping Dragon opened. A couple walked out and climbed into their SUV. He heard the sound of the LRT whispering along Crowchild Trail. Then the SUV's engine started. Frederick reached inside the front pouch of his black hoody. The weight of a Beretta with an illegal twenty-round magazine settled there. He pulled his gloved right hand out and touched his pants pocket. The spare magazine was there. Forty rounds would be more than enough, but he palmed another clip and tucked it in the back pocket of his jeans as he climbed out of the Infiniti.

"Pike ordered this one," Anan had said when he thought Frederick was out of earshot. Frederick had better-than-average hearing and never let on he had this advantage. In fact, he played hard of hearing, forcing people like Anan — the twenty-five-year-old who ran the operation, gave the orders, passed out cash and spoke for Pike — to speak louder than necessary. Everyone knew that Pike kept his hands clean so Anan would be left with bloody fingerprints if anything went wrong. Anan had been doing this kind of work before things went wrong for Moreau and Pike's brother, Stan. Anan was beginning to believe he was a survivor.

Not a good way to think in this business. Frederick took a long look around the parking lot. Only a black Land Rover and a white Escalade were parked in front of the restaurant.

He set pink earplugs in each ear, put on a balaclava, pulled his hood up, walked to the restaurant, put his hand around the butt of the Beretta and opened the door.

chapter 3

It was just eight a.m. when Lane saw the pictures on the metre-wide screen of his computer. The bodies were in a booth. Four male corpses propped up against one another and the wall, as if the victims believed leaning away from the shooter would offer them a better chance of survival. All four had been shot in the head. Two in the face, one in the side of the head and the last in the back of the head. No one else, including the lone waitress, the manager and the cook, had been injured. When they saw the man with the balaclava enter the front door, they retreated to the kitchen. Six shell casings and the handgun — a 9-mm Beretta with fourteen bullets remaining in the clip — had been left behind.

Detective Nigel Li sat in his chair behind the next desk. In large part because of his superior intelligence and fluency in multiple languages, Nigel was quick with a quip — or a jab — and had offended all of his former partners. He waited for Lane to analyze the scene.

Lane looked across at his partner. "How come you didn't call me last night?"

"Technically it was this morning." Nigel looked Lane in the eye. "There was no point in both of us seeing the brains on the wall."

Lane turned back to the pictures and shrugged. "Looks like the shooter left very little evidence."

Nigel inhaled and lifted his eyebrows. "The four victims are all known FKs — Fresh Off the Boat Killers."

"Do me a favour?" Lane got up and sat on the edge of his desk, crossed his arms and faced Nigel. Nigel had put on a few pounds since quitting boxing. He'd also allowed his black hair to grow out slightly, wore more colourful shirts and smiled more often since Anna had moved in with him. *He looks so much healthier now.*

"What's that?" Nigel sat up straighter.

"Quit trying to make my job easier."

Nigel glanced left.

Oh shit. "Lori's standing in the doorway, isn't she?"

"She is," Lori said.

Lane let his chin fall before he looked right. Lane and Li's loyal administrative assistant and de facto head of homicide Lori stood in the doorway with her arms crossed. As always she was impeccably put together. She wore a yellow blouse, black slacks and white pumps. Her hair was recently cut and styled, framing her face. *Is she letting some grey show?* Lane wondered.

"You've been a bit off ever since Christine, Dan and Indy moved out of your place," Lori said.

You always cut to the chase. "You've got me there." *What's the sense in denying it?*

"Well, I'd love to stand around and chat longer, but the Chief called and wants to see the pair of you."

Nigel sat up straight. "When?"

Lori backed out of the door. "Right now."

It took four minutes to get upstairs. Jean, the Chief's ever-present secretary with her close-cropped grey hair, white blouse and ready smile, nodded hello. "He's waiting for you." She got up and opened the door.

Calgary Police Service's new Chief Cameron Harper stood behind his desk looking out the window, his massive bear-like hands clasped behind his back. Harper was Lane's former partner and one of the few people the detective trusted besides Lori and Nigel. He was back in fighting trim at one hundred ninety pounds, but his short hair was receding and noticeably greyer than it had once been. He turned and waited for Nigel to close the door. "You guys need a coffee?"

"Sure." Nigel stood near one of the four chairs set around a knee-high oak coffee table.

He's worried he's going to piss Cam off again. Maybe there's hope for the two of them. Lane sat down in one of the chairs. "A coffee would be great."

Nigel sat down next to his partner while Harper pressed a button on his phone. "Could we please have four coffees? No phone calls." Cam sat next to Nigel and loosened his navy-blue tie as he crossed one uniformed leg over the other.

This can't be good.

Harper looked at Lane. "Indications are that we are about to have a gang war." He looked at Nigel. "What is said in this office stays here?"

Nigel nodded. "Of course."

"The Gang Suppression Unit is getting word that the FOBs — the Fresh Off the Boat gang — or the FKs are preparing for retaliation after yesterday's murders."

Nigel opened his mouth. "Yesterday's killings are atypical of either gang's tactics."

Lane cringed. Harper lifted his eyebrows. "How so?" He looked sideways at Lane.

"The killer acted alone. He left the gun behind and torched the car afterward. Those are not the usual tactics of either the FOBs or the FKs. They always work in pairs and up to this point have never left a weapon behind." Nigel looked at Lane and waited.

Lane turned to Harper. "What are you hearing?"

"It backs up what Nigel is saying. There's another player on the street making a move and trying to get the gangs to kill each other off so he can take over afterward."

Cam stood up as the door opened. Jean handed him a tray with four cups, a carafe of coffee, a pitcher of milk and a bowl of raw sugar. He set the tray down in the middle of the table.

Lane stared at the fourth cup.

Harper sat down, poured coffee into three of the cups and waited as each of them doctored their drinks. "We need to stop the war before it starts. If we don't, it's inevitable that innocents will be caught in the middle. I need information and I need it fast." He sipped his coffee, then used the cup to point at Lane. "And it looks like there's a connection with one of their suppliers from Culiacán."

Lane and Nigel leaned forward.

Harper continued. "Ignacio Fuentes thinks he owns the west coast of Mexico and is looking to establish markets in Canada for his product line. We're getting more reports of drug seizures at the Sweetgrass border crossing. The I-15 highway is seeing more drug traffic and so are Vancouver and Nanaimo."

"El Guapo," Nigel said.

"What?"

"Fuentes is called El Guapo. He was on the MCSC list. He's also supposed to be a chick magnet." Nigel took a sip of coffee.

"There's a meeting set for you two." Harper put his cup down and looked at Lane. "Chris Tuck wants to meet at eleven this morning. He's coming in from the Remand Center for X-rays. The medical office is on the fourth floor. You two will meet him on the third floor in an empty office." He handed Nigel a piece of paper with an address.

"What's he want from us?" Nigel asked.

"He says he has information. After the meeting, you two come back here and report what you've learned."

"He'll want something in return." *Tuck is to be sentenced after being convicted in two drive-bys. He's going away for at least twenty-five years — longer if he's classified as a dangerous offender.* Lane set his empty cup down and glanced at the carafe and unused cup. "Who else is coming to this meeting?"

"Arthur." Harper sat back and waited.

Lane pointed at his chest. "My Arthur?"

Harper nodded. "That's right. I have a favour to ask, and what we discuss with him also has to stay in this room." He looked pointedly at Nigel.

Nigel shrugged. "No problem."

There was a tap on the door. Harper got up, put his hand on Lane's shoulder and opened the door. "Thanks for coming on such short notice." He closed the door after Arthur stepped in. Arthur was dressed in casual blue slacks and an open-necked mauve shirt. He sat down in the empty chair. The incoming sun reflected off the top of his scalp. "Coffee?" Cam asked.

"No, thank you." Arthur smiled at Nigel. "How are you?"

"Good." Nigel frowned and looked nervously at Lane, who lifted his eyebrows. Sweat rolled from his armpits to his belt.

Harper sat and leaned forward with his elbows on his knees. "Erinn says that you two are thinking about a trip to Mexico."

"That's the plan." Arthur looked at Lane. *As usual, I'm the last to know when Arthur makes plans for us.*

"Most of the major players are meeting in Los Cabos next week. Bikers, Ignacio Fuentes and some of the other players are getting together. I think the Los Cabos meeting and this gang killing that you two —" he pointed at Lane and Nigel "— have inherited are related. I need someone down there to see what's what and who's involved." He turned to Lane. "How much of a beard can you grow by Monday?"

×

"Did you know Arthur was going to be there?" Nigel drove west on Crowchild Trail. The sun was low and the trees had lost their golds and oranges. Dead leaves collected against fences when the wind blew. Nigel eased onto the off ramp to Nose Hill Drive, then headed north toward Robert Thirsk High School. The grey-and-white brick building stood above the library and YWCA. Nigel turned left at the lights and headed instead for the four-storey office building facing south and west toward the mountains. The white on the peaks was edging its way down to the tree line, creeping inexorably back into the valleys, foothills and prairie. Nigel parked near the Treasury Branch. They walked up to the office building flanked by a liquor store and a dental office. Inside, they waited for the elevator and rode up to the third floor. They found the empty office and stepped inside. The ceiling tiles were gone, revealing air ducts, electrical lines and PVC pipe normally hidden by a suspended ceiling. Lane felt the dust and grit under his feet. A desk and three chairs sat near one of the windows. A man in orange coveralls perched on one of the chairs with his wrists and ankles shackled. Chris Tuck's red hair was cut close enough to reveal the scalp underneath. He studied the approaching detectives, his face wearing either a smirk or a smile.

Lane put his hand on his Glock, pulled a chair about a metre away from Chris and sat. Nigel stood to Lane's left.

"All right if we talk in private?" Tuck nodded at the beefy pair of guards in their blue Corrections uniforms.

Lane glanced at the men, who looked as if they worked out religiously. Their biceps were the size of some men's thighs. "Okay if you guys wait outside the door for a few minutes?"

The pair nodded and went out into the hallway.

"What kind of phone you got?" Chris looked at Nigel.

Nigel shook his head. "You said you had some information for us."

"You know about Melanie?" Chris's eyes shifted from one detective to the other and back again.

Lane recalled the name from Tuck's file. "Your sister?"

Chris nodded so enthusiastically that the chains on his cuffs rattled. "Yep. My little sister, she's thirteen."

I wonder if Tuck smiles when he kills? "And?"

"If I help you, I want you to get Melanie out of the city. Send her to my aunt and uncle's place. They live on the Island. She'll be safe there. Too much payback comin' around in this town." Chris kept smirking as he watched Lane.

Nigel pulled out his phone and began to tap in a few notes. *Nigel, what are you up to?*

Chris pointed at Nigel's phone. "I haven't seen one of those before. What does it do?"

"It has a bullshit app." Nigel looked up from his phone and smiled. "Stop wasting our time and get to the point or we're out of here." The smile remained.

Here we go!

"Just trying to make conversation. I get tired of talking to the same people all the time." The smirk never left Chris's face even though his eyes focused too long on Nigel.

"What's your sister's full name and address?" Nigel had his finger poised over the face of his phone.

Chris recited it.

Nigel entered the address. "What is your uncle's address in Duncan?" Nigel leaned back.

"How did you know he lives in Duncan?" Chris asked.

"I read your file. You spent a summer there after your first kill. What's the address?"

Chris gave it.

"Now what do you have for us?" Nigel looked up when he finished entering the address.

Lane sat back and watched Chris's eyes. They revealed

the shifting focus of a brain with a miniscule attention span and the ability to analyze situations rapidly.

"I know who yesterday's shooter is." Chris fiddled with his handcuffs. "These things get on my nerves."

"Well?" Lane waited for Chris to shift his focus.

"I want a chocolate milkshake first." Chris looked sideways at Nigel. "I've been dying for a DQ chocolate milkshake. That's part of the deal."

"Fuck off." Nigel looked at Lane. "I'm tired of being jerked around." He turned and moved toward the door.

"Frederick. The guy's name is Frederick. He lives with his parents. A delivery guy recognized the kid because Frederick goes to the same high school as his son." The smirk remained glued on Chris's face.

Nigel waited at the door. "What delivery guy and why should I believe you?"

Chris smiled and this time his eyes smiled as well. "I have better contacts than you do. My guy delivers fresh vegetables from a local greenhouse. He spotted Frederick in the restaurant parking lot when he dropped off some produce."

"Which high school does Frederick go to?" Lane asked.

Chris pointed out the window. "The one right over there."

Lane stood. "That's it, then."

Chris stood. "When I hear that Melanie is safe on the Island, then I'll tell you who's running Frederick."

Nigel walked over to the door, opened it, then slammed it shut. He turned on Chris. "We're not playing games with you. Either we get all you know right now or the deal's off."

Lane watched the smile on Chris's face. *He just never stops with the smiling.*

Chris held his cuffed hands together. "You won't believe me."

"Try us," Lane said.

"Sean Pike." Chris's eyes leapt from Lane to Nigel.

Nigel shook his head, opened the door and walked out.

Chris pointed at Lane and began to speak so quickly Lane had trouble following. "Sean Pike thinks you are the reason why his brother was killed, the reason why the woman who killed him was never charged. I'd watch out if I were you."

"Pike's dead." Lane heard the door open as the Corrections officers entered.

Chris laughed so hard he began to cough. He covered his mouth with his forearm pointing at Lane. "Yeah, right!" He lifted his chin, looking more predatory than before. "You're supposed to be this great detective. I can't believe how fuckin' gullible you are! You're unfinished business for Pike. He's the fuckin' Godfather, man!" Lane stepped out of the door as Chris hollered, "Dead man walkin'!" The door closed behind him.

$$\times$$

Lane and Nigel were hustled into Harper's office despite the frowns of senior officers already sitting and waiting. This time Cam leaned his backside against the front of his desk with his palms resting on the top. "What did you find out?"

"Besides the fact that Tuck is a bullshitter?" Nigel took a slow breath and waited for the inevitable blast from the Chief. When it didn't happen, he pointed at his partner. "He said Lane is in Pike's sights and we should look for a kid named Frederick at the local high school."

Harper nodded. "So he doesn't think Pike is dead?"

Nigel shook his head. "He gave us the impression that we would have to be stupid if we thought Pike was really dead."

"Who's the resource officer at Thirsk High School?" Lane asked.

Harper frowned and shook his head. "We need to keep this in this room. The officer at Thirsk, well, it would be . . .

We wouldn't want to tip off who you're looking for." He shook his head and looked at Nigel. "Do you have a way of accessing the Calgary Board of Education's records?"

Nigel looked at Lane, then at Harper. "I do."

Harper said, "The Resource Officer at Thirsk is one of Smoke's good ol' boys."

"I can get Anna to check it out." Nigel looked out the window at the blue sky.

Harper turned to Lane. "So Pike is alive?"

Lane shrugged. "Tuck seemed certain that Pike was still in the game."

"Not much of a surprise, really." Harper rubbed his face with his palm.

"I don't think so. I still want to go to Los Cabos and see what's up." Lane looked at Nigel when he raised his eyebrows.

"I'm not sure how." Harper pushed himself away from the desk.

"You forget how good I am at blending in." Lane smiled.

Nigel said, "In Mexico a *fresa* stands out like a turd in a hot tub."

Harper laughed and Nigel's eyes opened wide.

"That depends on how many fresas are in the tub," Lane said.

chapter 4

"There is a Frederick Lee in grade twelve at Thirsk. The other possibility is a Fred Robertson and he's in grade ten." Nigel sat at his desk and pointed at the message on his screen.

"Can you send me the pictures? I'll put them on the map." Lane opened up his email and waited for the message.

Nigel tapped a few keys. "Lee is getting top grades. Robertson is a solid C. Neither has an arrest record."

Lane downloaded the pictures and placed Fred and Frederick side by side next to a picture of the Sleeping Dragon restaurant. "How long will it take to get detailed profiles on both? I'd like to look over any comments made on their report cards."

"Anna sent those too. On their way now." Nigel pressed a key and leaned back in his chair.

Lane waited for the message to arrive, then opened it and began to read.

✕

"Your essays are due on Tuesday," Ms. Baker reminded her students as she glanced at the classroom clock.

Frederick's phone vibrated in his pocket. He pulled the phone out and read the text. 11:30 *tonight at the Caboose*. The bell rang. Frederick stood, picked up his books and walked out the door. Despite the Friday afternoon crush, at least a metre remained between him and the people in front and behind.

In the hallway, eyes looked away when they saw Frederick approaching. He hid a smile behind a blank expression and walked down the centre of the hallway in a bubble of private space. One gangly grade ten boy was talking to a friend and did not see Frederick. The boy's friend grabbed him by the arm. The boy's spotted face turned white when he saw Frederick just before they avoided colliding.

Up ahead, a clutch of football players approached in black leather team jackets. Each of them outweighed Frederick by at least fifty pounds. He walked directly toward them. They parted, and he passed through a cloud of aftershave and body wash, his eyes watering. He blinked as he walked out the rear door and into the parking lot. His black Mercedes M-class SUV sat in its regular parking spot. He climbed in the right-hand side and set his books on the passenger seat. He started the engine, turned the heater on high, then checked his look in the mirror. His black hair was trimmed close on the sides, gelled Elvis on top; his skin was clear, face round and eyes brown.

There was a knock on the passenger window. He looked left and saw Brittany. Her blonde hair was tied back and she wore a black bustier under a red leather jacket, skintight red jeans, red leather knee-high boots and the gold necklace he'd bought her last week. He opened the door and picked up his books; she sat down with her voluminous Gucci purse. "Some day I'll get used to getting in on the wrong side."

"The right side in Japan." He tossed his books onto the back seat and looked out the tinted windows. He noted surreptitious glances aimed his way from passersby.

Brittany closed her door, set her purse on the floor and put on her seat belt. "I can't believe how cheap a Mercedes is when you ship it in from Japan."

Frederick shifted into reverse and shoulder checked. "I have to work tonight."

Brittany flicked her hair, then turned to focus on him with her green eyes. "But I made a reservation."

"Cancel it."

Lane held the phone and nodded while Nigel waved him over with one hand and pointed at the computer screen with the other.

Arthur said, "We're ready to go. Just need to drop by Mountain Equipment Co-op to pick up a few things." Lane stuck his left finger in his ear while Arthur continued talking into his right. He looked around the office. *How the hell will we get everything done by Monday?* "There's something else." Arthur hesitated. "We're going out for dinner with Christine, Dan, Indiana and Matt."

"And?"

"With Lola and John and their daughter Linda. Apparently Linda insists on meeting us."

Lane took a long breath. "When?"

"Tomorrow night." Arthur hung up.

"You look pissed." Nigel rubbed an itchy nose. "Look at this."

Lane put his phone down and shifted to his partner's desk. Nigel pointed at his screen. "In grade ten, Frederick Lee transferred to Thirsk after two months at Winston Churchill. I wonder why?"

×

Brittany stopped in front of a window at Market Mall. The sprawling shopping centre was filled with mall-walking seniors, pregnant moms with metre-wide strollers and shoppers stalking deals. This store had a pair of knee-high boots in its window. The polished red leather shone under the spotlights; the stitching was blue as were the soles. She looked at him and raised her eyebrows.

Ten minutes later they left the shoe store. Brittany was wearing a new pair of boots. They checked out at five hundred fifty dollars. Her old boots were in the box under Frederick's arm. "I need a cup of coffee," he said, turning in the direction of the elevator to the basement parking lot.

He was halfway through the caramel macchiato by the time they stepped off the elevator and into the underground parkade. Frederick handed his girlfriend the keys to the Mercedes. "You drive it to your place. I need to have a look around. I'll meet you there."

Brittany studied him, her head tipped to one side. "What kind of work do you have to do?"

Frederick shook his head. He walked to the front of his black Mercedes, then toward the cars parked at the far end of the underground lot. The exhaust fans hummed as they pumped in fresh air. Tires chirped on the polished concrete surface and there was an intermittent echo of doors and trunks being shut. He spotted a woman loading a toddler into a stroller. The little girl wore pink leggings and a rainbow glitter top made of purple cotton. The mother strapped the child in, put her purse over her shoulder and walked away pushing the stroller. Next to her, a woman stuck her keys in the trunk of a candy-apple-red Mustang and retrieved a parcel. She shut the trunk and walked away. Her three-inch heels telegraphed her progress toward the elevator. Frederick glanced at the keys dangling from the lock and waited until the woman disappeared inside the elevator. He walked to the Mustang, pulled out the keys, got in, adjusted the seat and mirror, started the engine and motored out of the underground parking and into the sunlight.

✕

"Try this on." Arthur held out a long-sleeved lightweight shirt. He and Lane were standing in front of a wall of shirts on the second floor of the Mountain Equipment Co-op — MEC, as the locals called it.

"It's kind of bland." Lane regarded the green shirt's front pockets and side vents skeptically.

"This isn't about fashion. It's about looking like a fresa so people don't look closely at your face." Arthur shook his head. "And people say *I'm* a princess!"

"Do I have to wear a big camera around my neck, too?" *Shit! He's right. I am beginning to sound like a princess!*

Arthur rolled his eyes and handed Lane the shirt. "Just try it on." He reached over and lifted a pair of khaki-coloured shorts off the rack. "And these."

"Anything else? A fanny pack, perhaps?" Lane took the clothing and looked over his shoulder for the location of the changing room.

"Any more sarcasm from you and it'll be socks and sandals on the beach."

A forty-something woman in dreads, a T-shirt and baggy khaki pants walked by. "I went to a resort like that. Everyone wore sandals and nothing else!"

Lane and Arthur waited until she turned a corner, lifting their eyebrows at the same time. Lane said, "And I'm not wearing one of those stupid floppy old-fart hats with the string under the chin!"

×

Frederick parked about thirty metres away from the front door of the Caboose. It was a pizza and rib restaurant, the latest eatery in a cluster of strip malls with a parking lot in the middle and furniture, electronics and department stores on each of the four sides of the square. The Caboose was on the inside of one corner. Its decor was accented by one faux brick wall providing the impression it had, at one time, been a train station. The door was set in between railings and under the lip of a peaked roof with Caboose written across the top.

Frederick knew his prey was inside because he had parked next to the target's white Range Rover. All Frederick had to do was wait for the party of four to walk out the Caboose's front door. He reached into his jacket pocket, pulled out blue surgical gloves and snapped them on. Then he used his right hand to pick up the Beretta on the passenger seat. He caught a glimpse of a red Dodge pickup truck poised on oversized tires when it passed in front of him. Frederick lifted his eyes to watch the front door of the restaurant. He heard the truck's engine recede then return.

Four headlights shone in the Mustang's rear-view mirror. Frederick looked out of his side mirror. The passenger door of the truck opened. A pair of boots dropped below the open door and touched the pavement.

Frederick reached for the keys and started the Mustang. He saw the tip of the barrel of a long gun rising from the vertical to the horizontal. He shifted into drive, jammed his foot onto the throttle and cranked the wheel to the left.

The first blast from the shotgun punched a fist-sized hole through the metal panel behind the driver's door. Frederick straightened the wheel, the car's tail end slid around and he swung the wheel to the right. The second blast made a volleyball-sized hole in the passenger door glass before he could steer around the corner of the building.

Frederick tucked the Beretta under his right thigh. He ran the red light and turned left. Then he reached for his seat belt. Pinpricks of pain were dancing their stiletto heels on his right shoulder. Adrenalin made him jittery. He glanced in his rear-view mirror as he accelerated along Country Hills Boulevard, took the long curve to join the freeway and headed south on Stoney Trail. The four headlights of the pickup truck were about three hundred metres behind him. Frederick looked ahead. Traffic was light. He eased off the accelerator, estimating the pickup would catch up to him before they reached the bridges connecting Stoney and Crowchild Trails. He tested his left shoulder and arm, felt the muscles moving freely. Then he gripped the wheel with his left hand and checked his right shoulder and arm. The pain was becoming intense, but his arm and fingers still moved. He glanced at the speedometer. One hundred and forty kilometres per hour. The wind buffeted against the holes blasted by the shotgun. He looked again in the rear-view mirror. The truck was gaining. It passed under a streetlight and he noted how high it sat on its oversized wheels. Frederick nodded as the vehicles began the descent into the Bow River valley. Ahead, the moon and city lights illuminated both sides of the valley. He switched open the driver-side window and grabbed the wheel with his left hand and the Beretta with his right. The wind clutched at his shirt and hair.

The truck bore down on him. He saw the barrel of a gun poking out the passenger window. The truck was within twenty metres. Frederick's right foot stomped the brake pedal. Several things happened at once.

The truck's passenger fired and missed. Frederick aimed, fired twice and hit the truck's rear tire on the passenger side. The pickup swerved, the driver overcorrected, tires howled and the Dodge swung the other way.

Frederick aimed for the far left-hand side of the road. He accelerated along the driver's side of the pickup, fired one round through the Mustang's shattered passenger window into the truck's front tire. He pushed his foot to the floor. The engine shifted down and roared. He grimaced at the pain when his wounded shoulder was shoved against the seat back. He moved into the right lane then glanced in the rear-view. The truck was cartwheeling, shedding bits of metal, plastic, glass, rubber and a body as it disintegrated.

chapter 5

Frederick looked over his right shoulder at the mirror and dabbed white antibiotic cream on his angry red wounds. He'd kept the four pellets the nurse had dug one by one out of his shoulder; he looked at them now sitting at the bottom of a glass half filled with alcohol, the normally clear liquid pink with his blood. He'd left the silent nurse five hundred-dollar bills on the counter of her "after-hours" clinic in a house just west of Centre Street north near 30th Avenue.

×

Lane sat down across from Christine. She studied him with her brown eyes but did not smile or speak. Indiana, on the other hand, smiled broadly, drooled on his rainbow T-shirt then pounded on the table with his rubber teething ring. They sat under the Italian restaurant's photograph of a Napolitano man kissing the cheek of a beautifully reluctant woman who even in black and white exuded tired tolerance of the man with the bristly cheeks. Lane scratched his own cheek. The bristles were getting long enough to change the shape of his face. He looked at the pizza oven door where orange flames were glowing at the back. *This could be a long dinner.* He turned back to Christine's husband Dan, who raised his eyebrows and gave a brief smile.

They heard her before she spoke. The three-inch heels of her red leather knee-high boots announced her arrival like a drum beat on the plank floor. "There you are!" Lola put her hands on Arthur's shoulders. He stood and gave her a hug. Lola's husband John shook hands with Lane.

Dan and Christine remained seated. Lane saw that Lola wore red pants, a red blouse and a white leather coat. Her hair and eyebrows had been dyed blonde. Someone had applied her makeup. Her lipstick was a glossier shade than her red blouse.

Lane felt a gentle hand on his shoulder. "Hello there, I'm Linda." He turned to his right and saw a woman in her late twenties or early thirties. She was as tall as Dan and had her father's gentle green eyes, auburn hair and perfect teeth; she also had a broad smile. She held out her arms. He got a pleasing whiff of subtle floral perfume and raspberry-scented shampoo. Lane stood, and Linda hugged him as he introduced Arthur. She released Lane and waited for Arthur. Linda hugged then released Arthur before reaching for Christine, Indiana and her brother. The siblings exchanged a genuine embrace. Linda walked around the table and sat next to her brother.

The waiter wore a white shirt and black pants, and his black hair was slicked back. "Would you like to order some drinks?"

After he left with their drink orders, Christine got up to carry Indiana over to the glass separating the wood oven from the patrons. Indiana watched the flames inside the oven then locked onto the restored Vespa parked nearby.

Linda leaned closer to Dan and made eye contact with Lane. "It's good to finally meet you. I was working in the States when the wedding happened and try as I might, there was no way the company I was working for would allow me to visit Cuba — they are, after all, ardent capitalists. Now I work for another investment firm and that means I travel from place to place checking out companies and countries they want to invest with, including Cuba." She pointed at Lane. "I insist on buying dinner, so order whatever you feel like. I head out tomorrow. I hear you're headed to Mexico on Monday."

Arthur said, "Just the two of us."

Christine sat back down. Lane gazed at Indiana's round face, close-cropped hair and two front teeth and felt a longing he couldn't contain. He reached out. Indiana smiled and extended his arms. Lane stood up, moved closer to Christine and waited. She waited several seconds before handing the toddler to Lane. Indiana tucked his head into Lane's neck, sniffed, farted and touched the stubble on Lane's face. Lane smiled and sat down. Minutes later Indiana was asleep, and Lane felt a warm sense of calm. He watched Christine, who continued to avoid eye contact. Still, he felt her glance at him once or twice when he was looking away.

Marco the waiter returned with their drinks. After each beverage was in place he asked, "Ready to order?"

After Marco left again, Lane studied the interactions around him. He noted the easy way Linda chatted with her brother. Lola perched, interrupting them with questions answered with one or two words before the siblings continued their catching up. Christine leaned into Dan. Arthur and Matt commented on the illuminated black-and-white photographs on the wall, discussing possible stories behind the portraits.

"Indiana sure seems to like you." Linda raised a glass of wine and saluted the detective. She turned to Christine. "How do you like the new place?"

Christine leaned forward. "It's nice to have our own space."

Lola said, "We're giving it to them rent free!"

Linda looked at her mother. Dan blushed as he looked at his father and then at Indiana.

Lola said, "We're helping out. They were living with Arthur and Lane. It was a little crowded."

Lane heard the condescension in Lola's tone.

Linda turned to her mother. "What exactly are you saying, Mother?"

Lola looked at John, then at her son. "Just sharing some information with family, that's all." She lifted her hands palms up as if in hurt surrender. She looked to John for sympathy.

Matt coughed and looked at Christine, whose eyes went black as she gazed over Lane's head.

The waiter arrived with a pizza and a calzone. He set them down in front of Lola and Linda. The other pizzas and calzones arrived moments later. Lola used a knife to quarter her pizza.

Lane used his right hand to cut off the crusty end of his calzone, then dripped some chili oil on the bread. Arthur leaned over and cut a couple of bite-sized strips from Lane's calzone. Lane balanced Indiana and listened to his deep breathing. He speared a sliver of calzone, saw it ooze mozzarella, tomato sauce, olive oil and meat. The scent made him drool. He put the first bite in his mouth, closed his eyes and leaned his head so that his chin touched Indiana. *I've really missed you, little one.*

Lola waved at the waiter. "This is not what I ordered!"

The waiter came over. "I'm sorry, madam. What did you order?"

"The calzone." Lola pointed at Matt's plate.

Matt blushed as he chewed.

The waiter picked up Lola's pizza. "I'll be right back with your calzone."

"You ordered a pizza, Mom," Dan said.

Lola glared at him. "I ordered a calzone!"

Linda looked at Christine, then back at Lane. She leaned forward to confide in Lane. "I heard you are the hero who saved four lives and tracked down a pair of serial killers."

Lane felt the eyes of the others on him and looked again at the picture of the woman reluctantly accepting a kiss.

Linda's asking you a question. He lowered his eyes, chewed and swallowed. "I did my job."

Linda continued to study Christine. "Dan said you and Christine were very close up until about a month before they moved into the condo."

There's no artifice to Linda. And there's a tension between her and her Lola. This might get interesting.

Christine shrugged, then lifted her napkin and wiped at her eyes. Lane saw two smudges of mascara on the white fabric. He glanced at Lola, who looked away.

Linda looked across the table at Lola. "What have you been up to?"

Lola leaned back in her chair. "Me? Nothing."

Linda looked at Lane. "What did she do?"

The pause lasted at least twenty seconds and seemed to be reaching toward infinity.

Arthur leaned to his right and glanced at Lola, pointing with his fork at her to underline his words. "You told Paul that you didn't want your grandson growing up in the home of a killer."

Lane heard a collective inhalation. He turned to look at Dan, whose eyes were focused on his mother. Then Lane looked at Christine, who was staring back at him.

Christine asked, "She said that to you?"

Lane nodded.

"And you believed it?" Christine's voice cracked.

"I ..." Lane shook his head then looked at Linda whose eyes were boring into her mother's.

Lola put her hands up. "I said no such thing! And I didn't come here to be accused of something I didn't do." She looked at her son. "We gave you a rent-free condo!"

Lane heard an electronic click. He looked at Arthur, who had set a handheld recorder on the table. "How'd you get that?"

Arthur said, "Lori gave it to me. This recording may clarify a few things."

Matt savoured a mouthful of calzone with a hint of a smile as he watched the drama unfold.

Lola's voice was the first one they heard on the recording. "John and I have spoken, and we feel that Dan, Christine and Indiana need a place of their own."

"That's what you've decided?" Lane's voice asked.

"We offered them one of our condominiums rent free."

There was a pause; then Lola's voice continued. "I've been concerned for Indiana's safety because of your work. Matt was kidnapped as a result of your choice of profession and you must agree that Indiana's safety is a priority. It's best for them if they have a safe place to raise their family. And I have some very personal concerns."

"They are?" Lane's voice asked.

"My grandson is growing up in the home of a killer. Of course what you did was legal, but I think you will agree, if you look at the situation dispassionately, that Indiana's psychological needs would be better served in an environment free from the inevitable aftermath of such an event. Besides, he needs a more traditional family environment. Have you anything to say?"

There was the sound of a door opening and Nigel's voice said, "Sorry."

Arthur stopped the tape and pocketed the recorder. "That's it."

Linda glared at Lola. "You always did say the end justifies the means, Mother."

Lola sat up straight and leaned her head back. "I did what needed to be done to protect my grandson!"

"My son!" Christine snapped. She turned to Dan. "Our son!" She turned back to Lola. "Cut the bullshit, Lola. You only do what's good for you!"

Lola pointed a finger at Christine. "It's always the newest member of a family who causes the problems!"

Lane felt the heat rise toward his forehead then to his hairline.

Linda laughed. "Have another drink of wine, Mother. You're just trying to shift the blame."

Lola stood up. Her chair fell backwards. She pointed at Dan, then at Christine. "You'd better get that one under control!"

Lane stood up. *Keep your voice low. Your words need to be slow, calculated.* "Christine is doing just fine. You're the one who's out of control."

Indiana woke up and began to whimper. Lane rubbed the boy's back.

Lola poked Lane's arm with her manicured index finger. "Now look at what you've done!" She picked up her purse, turned and swung Gucci over her shoulder. The purse swung wide, forcing the approaching waiter to duck. Lola's heels pounded over the wooden planks. The sound was magnified by the silence. Her husband took deep a breath and looked around the table, mouthing *Sorry* at Dan before following his wife.

Christine was watching Lane as he sat back down and rocked Indiana, who slipped back to sleep.

The waiter stood with Lola's calzone for a moment until Linda said, "Please set it there." She pointed at Lola's empty place setting. "Drama can be good for the appetite."

"Why didn't you tell us?" Christine asked.

Lane shrugged.

"He had to shoot that guy," Matt said. "He *had* to. He didn't *want* to. What else could he have done to stop those killers?"

Linda smiled at the waiter. "Could we take a look at the wine list, please?" She looked at Dan, who was staring at the untouched food on his plate. Linda put her hand on his back. "Let's get this party started. We both know what she's like. Now that she's gone we can relax and enjoy each other's company. I've missed you, brother, and I absolutely adore my nephew and sister-in-law."

×

Lane's phone buzzed as he put it down on the kitchen table. He tapped a button and a message from Nigel filled the screen. *Two FOBs dead on Stoney Trail. Shotgun and handgun recovered at the scene. Stolen Mustang recovered fifteen minutes ago in Ramsey. Two holes in vehicle. Blood sample recovered.*

Lane leaned against the counter. *Harper was right. This could be the beginning of a gang war.*

chapter 6

The sun was up. Lane looked through the glass and across the airport apron where a pair of WestJet blue tails pointed at the sky. He looked left at the Fur Trader's Hut where moccasins, leather jackets, wooden snowshoes, a moose head, a ceramic bear and other assorted *authentic* Canadiana awaited sale. A black-haired, almond-skinned woman sat behind the till and spoke on her cell phone. "What do you want me to do? I'm at work. The chai is on the shelf above the stove!"

Arthur tapped Lane's forearm. "Still full from last night?"

Up to this point, they had been quiet about last night's dinner conversation. *It's a lot to digest*, Lane thought.

A woman said, "I thought it needed to be out there so I put it out there."

Sharp, cackling laughter erupted from a group sitting two rows away in the departure area. Lane looked over his shoulder. One woman wore a straw cowboy hat with a rolled-up brim. Her mouth was wide and her teeth were unnaturally white. There was a rasp of hard liquor and cigarettes in her laughter. The woman next to her wore a Flames jersey and shoulder-length, black-dyed hair that she pushed back with fluorescent pink nails. After the look-at-me laughter died down, Lane said, "I thought we had a good visit after Lola left. Linda wasn't what I expected. She sure has Lola figured out."

"Linda seems determined to keep as much distance as possible from her mother. Dan told me Linda took the job in the States to get some breathing space from Lola. Linda initially talked about living in Australia." Arthur watched as the luggage was loaded onto their aircraft.

"It was good to see Indiana and Christine again." Lane remembered how wet the shoulder of his shirt was when he handed the baby back to his mother.

"She actually talked to you. That's a step in the right direction."

Lane smiled. "Yes, she asked me, 'So you listened to her bullshit?'"

Arthur laughed so loud it momentarily drowned out the noise from Straw Hat and Pink Nails. He put his hand on Lane's knee. "That's one of the many nice things about our Christine. She always gets right to the point!"

They were alone on the beach. The moon spilled silver onto the black water of the Sea of Cortez and waves crashed white against the sand. The stars were thick in the black when Arthur took Lane's hand. They turned back to La Luna Cortez, an orange-stuccoed four-storey resort structure in the shape of a U. The open ends pointed at the ocean and the middle of the U shaded a meandering pool framed with palm trees. "When do we get to work?" Arthur asked.

Lane pointed at a gathering of men who sat near the pool where blue-and-white lounge chairs had been pulled into a circle. Nearby, a quartet of bodyguards surveyed the grounds. "Looks like we've already started."

The meandering pathway leading to Arthur and Lane's main-floor room brought them close to one of the guards. Arthur stepped in front of Lane, who put his hand on his partner's shoulder.

One of the bodyguards, wearing a black T-shirt, pants and shoes, spotted them and said, "*Maricóns!*"

All of the others turned to survey Lane and Arthur. There was a flash of teeth then general dismissive laughter before the guards turned away.

It's likely they will no longer pay us the slightest bit of attention, Lane thought as he caught the spicy aromas of testosterone and Cuban tobacco on the breeze.

chapter 7

Lane sat down near the cappuccino bar in the cavernous lobby of La Luna Cortez. A young woman approached him. She wore a white blouse and black skirt and her black hair was tied back. She squeaked closer on soft soles. "Café?"

Lane read her nametag and asked, "Cappuccino, *por favor*, Lucy?"

Lucy nodded and walked away.

He opened his laptop, logged onto the hotel's WiFi and looked out at the bougainvillea, the palm trees and the pool where a pair of young women in bikinis and oversized sombreros were pouring tequila down the throat of a thirsty thirty-ish male in a black Speedo. Lane's inbox opened up and he saw Christine's name. He aimed the cursor and read.

Uncle Lane,

I hope you and Arthur are enjoying your holiday.

I thought that maybe by writing you I could tell you how I've felt the last few months. Hearing what Lola said to you has made me think about what happened between us and the way you've shut yourself off from us.

Actually, I want to scream and say, "How stupid could you be listening to what Lola says?!" Maybe that's why it's better for us to communicate this way. I can think before I speak.

Matt and Arthur told me that Lola knows how to spot a scar and scratch at it until it opens up again. I've begun to believe it's true. Linda told me as much last night. We talked in the car on the way to her hotel. She said she went to university in Halifax to get away from Lola. She said that after two years of taking some psychology courses, she was able to see her mother for what she is. The words Linda used were "pathetic," "self-absorbed" and "controlling." She thinks her mother needs to feel powerful. But the reasons why Lola acts the way she does don't really matter. Linda also said something very interesting. "My mother can only control you and manipulate you if you let her. Once you become aware of her personality and acquire some objectivity, you realize that she can only have power over you if you let her."

I think that's what you and I need to learn. We have allowed Lola to control us, to influence us. To scratch the scars off of old wounds.

What I'm trying to say is that Indiana needs you and so do I. What do you say?

Love,

Christine

×

Lane walked the beach. He wore knee-length black shorts, a long-sleeved blue shirt, a ball cap and sunglasses. Arthur waited at the side of the pool for Fuentes and his entourage to appear. Lane felt the firm wet sand under his feet. He noted the gold flecks in the white and looked ahead to see a man standing inland on a sand dune. He held a three-metre fishing pole. The line stretched over Lane's head. The fisherman in the ball cap, red shirt and jeans yanked back on the rod to set the hook, then began to wind the reel. In less than thirty seconds a silver fish with a yellow fin was dangling from the line about a foot below the tip of the rod.

Lane walked on as the waves rolled in. Ahead he spotted a trio of men looking out at the Sea of Cortez. He turned and peered toward the horizon. A whale's tail slapped the water. There was a spout of spray as another exhaled. A third whale smacked the water with a pectoral fin. Then a whale launched itself out of the water and tipped sideways to fall back into the sea with a splash breaking the horizon's grey line.

Lane stood waiting for the whales to breach again. A wave rolled up onto the beach and reached halfway to his knees. He remembered the kokanee as they swam upstream in answer to their instinctive drive to spawn, turning the fresh water to orange gold. Here the whales practised a ritualistic dance they had refined over centuries. Before recorded history, they had travelled here in the winter and to the Bering Sea in the summer. Lane, ever the hunter, was hypnotized by them and wondered why kokanee, whales and people alike seemed unable to break the pattern of their behaviours. Was it nature or nurture? Was it woven into their very DNA?

A pair of boats appeared close to the whales as they continued their performance. A cigarette boat with its long bow, open cockpit and throbbing engine aimed itself at the whales. There was an intermittent crackle of gunfire. The whales ceased their breaching and tail slapping. The cigarette boat's engine roared and the boat accelerated toward Puerto Los Cabos. Waves splashed from its bow. The others on the beach turned to one another wide-eyed, as if seeking confirmation of what they had just witnessed.

chapter 8

Christine,

I know it was stupid of me to allow Lola's comments to get under my skin. The simple fact is that they did. It is difficult to explain how killing Andrew Pierce has fundamentally affected my perceptions of the world and myself. I believed what separated me from the people I hunted was not being a killer. Becoming a killer has tipped me off balance.

I think that you and Linda and Arthur are correct. Lola has a gift for sensing weaknesses and exploiting them. Her LOLAGETS licence plate is very revealing. It is so obviously a clue to understanding her that I missed it at first. Her main focus is getting what she wants.

I also think you and Linda are right. She has power over us only if we allow that to happen.

As far as apologies go, I can only hope you will accept mine. I was wrong to fall for such an obvious ploy. I should never have allowed so much time to pass without apologizing to you.

Love,

Your Uncle

×

Lane lifted his right foot onto the bathroom counter and lathered aloe vera onto his red pepper sunburned skin. He shifted feet and did the other.

"How are they?" Arthur asked.

Lane looked at his partner's reflection in the mirror. Arthur's Lebanese skin was darker. A bit of puffiness around the eyes was the only indication they had spent about the same amount of time in yesterday's Mexican sun. "Sore, but they'll be okay by tomorrow. My own fault for not putting on sunscreen before standing out there and watching the whales."

"They were magnificent, though."

"Can't believe those guys in the cigarette boat were shooting at them." Lane washed his hands and wiped them on the towel. "Ready for breakfast?" He slipped his feet into sandals and winced.

There was a knock at the door. Arthur opened it. A round woman in a grey housekeeping uniform stood as tall as the cart she pushed. Her nametag read Elena. "Cleaning?"

Arthur smiled. "We were just going out for breakfast." He reached in his shirt pocket and handed her US dollars. The men left.

They went out into the sun next to the pool. Beyond the stone wall and toward the horizon, the sea reflected the sun's light off its back. Waves rolled onto the beach, pounding a drumbeat. Lane and Arthur walked around the bar then to the cafeteria where the maître d' directed them to a table. The room had a high ceiling, murals of colourful rural Mexican life on the walls and a view of the ocean. Lane sat and waited for coffee while Arthur went to fill his plate. Lane spotted Fuentes at a long table where five children under ten years sat, ate and squirmed. Fuentes fed the youngest, a boy with thick black hair and a red T-shirt. A thirty-something woman sat at the middle of the table between twin girls with braided hair. At the far end another, younger woman sat and ate slowly while avoiding eye contact with Fuentes. He sat with his perfect whitened teeth, carefully coiffed black hair, chiseled chin and aquiline nose.

Arthur set his plate down. It was a colourful collection of fresh baked banana bread, pineapple, honeydew melon, strawberries, fried plantains and yogurt. "Your turn."

The waiter arrived with a carafe of coffee and filled their cups. Lane glanced to the left.

Arthur asked, "Want me to keep my eyes open?"

Lane nodded, got up and walked toward the buffet. Moving down the steps, he surveyed the layout. Omelettes were being prepared on his right and left. In the centre were two lines of hot trays under glass where people crowded around a hill of bacon. In the middle was fresh fruit; on his left, a chef preparing tacos. He went for an omelettes and filled a bowl with fresh corn, peas, mushrooms and cilantro.

Heads turned. A woman with shimmering black hair, wearing a flowing silvery-blue silk dress, four-inch silver heels and a gold necklace, walked off a Paris runway and stepped into line in front of him. The woman preparing the omelettes wore a white uniform, apron and cap; her nametag said Mercedes. Lane opened his mouth to say something to the supermodel. Mercedes avoided looking at her; instead, she gave Lane an apologetic smile. Lane closed his mouth and watched. Supermodel picked out her choices, handed them to Mercedes, then flicked her Cher hair with her free hand as she surveyed the room with practised detachment.

From behind her, Lane observed the reactions to Supermodel's appearance. Some of the older Americans and Canadians stopped and stared. The Latinos took quick glances at her from a safe distance. *That is not normal. The men should be puffing out their chests and trying to make eye contact or offering assistance.*

Mercedes blushed when Supermodel departed, blushing again as she prepared Lane's omelette. She even went so far as to say, *"Muchas gracias, señor,"* as she handed him the plate and he sprinkled the omelette with salsa. He returned to the table and sat across from Arthur, who asked, "What happened?"

Lane shrugged as he cut into the omelette with his fork and began to eat. Out of the corner of his eye he saw Fuentes frown as the woman in blue silk passed, leaving a wake of pungent perfume and stiletto staccato on her way to the deck where the morning sun glared at the ocean.

Lane and Arthur spent much of the day on the patio watching the comings and goings of tourists and staff while distorted music blasted from a pair of inadequate speakers near the pool. A group of Canadians, clad in ball caps, straw cowboy hats, beards and black muscle shirts, drank and laughed with their wives. Their voices grew louder, causing nearby families to leave. Fuentes and his family spent the day poolside with a minor army of attendants who fetched towels, drinks and food.

Lane later wondered what would have happened if he hadn't had insomnia that night.

chapter 9

The clock read 3:11 when Lane woke with his senses on alert, his mind running a ten-kilometre race. He decided to take a walk in the cool warmth of the early morning. Arthur snored in the other queen bed. Lane pulled on shorts and a shirt but when his sunburned feet smarted at the touch of leather, decided against the sandals. He stuffed the key and his iPhone in his shirt pocket, grabbed a bottle of water from the fridge and slipped out the door.

He turned right and walked the hundred-metre hallway leading to the lobby. Along the way, he passed the children's play area where a pirate ship and a variety of brightly painted mammals posed. His nose reacted to the obscene stench of blood and shit. He turned his head to the left and looked though a half-moon portal. In the open mouth of the whale was the body of a woman in a blue silk dress and silver four-inch heels. Her skirt was pulled up over her waist, her legs were open and a black thong covered her Brazilian-waxed vulva. Shit slid down the tongue of the whale and mixed with the blood meandering into the wading pool beyond the tip of the whale's tongue. There was a line beneath the woman's chin, a wound stretching from under one looped earring to the other. He saw something sparkling in the open mouth of the wound: she still wore her gold necklace.

Lane looked left and right along the pool level hallway. *No footprints on the tiled floor.* He looked back at the woman and her open eyes. His right hand tapped his shirt pocket. He picked out his phone and took three quick photos of the body. He walked on tiptoes to the end of the corridor, past the slide, past the camel, the buffalo and the well-hung lion and looked at the glass door leading to the children's playground. One word was painted on the door in hand-drawn red letters: LOVE.

He turned away from the door and walked along the corridor as it took one ninety-degree turn then another before reaching the elevators. He pressed the button and waited for the doors to open completely before he stepped inside and used his knuckle to press L for the lobby. Again he waited for the doors to open wide before stepping out one floor above pool level, walking along the hallway leading to the lobby and wondering whether anyone would be working the front desk. He spotted a bald man in a green jacket crested with the white La Luna Cortez logo standing behind a computer monitor. The glass of the man's white-framed lenses reflected blue. Lane looked down at his own swollen red feet then walked up to the desk. He put his hands on the counter and read the man's nametag. "Ruben?"

The man's brown eyes lifted and took Lane in. "Si?"

Lane took a breath and forced himself to talk slowly. "A woman has been murdered and her body is in the mouth of the whale in the children's playground."

Ruben frowned as if he were doing an English-to-Spanish translation of what Lane had just told him.

"You speak English?"

Ruben nodded and pushed his glasses up. Lane could see sweat on the man's bald scalp. Ruben said, "My manager is coming."

"What about the police? Have you called them?" *Something is off here.*

The man was near pleading when he said, "My manager told me to —" he held his hand to his ear mimicking a phone "— call his friend from the ambulance company." He looked around. "My manager is coming."

An ambulance pulled up just outside the sliding glass front doors. Two men in white uniforms took a gurney out of the back.

Lane looked at Ruben. *You already knew about the body.*

Ruben read Lane's reaction and shrugged. "It's Mexico."

The doors whispered open. With a nod to Ruben, the men rolled the gurney across the white marble floor and headed for the elevators. A few minutes later, they rolled the gurney back along the hallway. A black body bag was strapped to the gurney. The ambulance attendants acted as if Lane and Ruben did not exist. The doors slipped opened and they rolled the gurney outside. They loaded the body in the back of the ambulance and were gone. Lane turned to Ruben. He was sweating despite the coolness of the evening, his brown eyes magnified by the lenses. His pupils were dilated. They told Lane all that he needed to know. *This murder is going to be hushed up and hidden away.*

He went down one floor, returned to the room for his laptop then walked barefoot back to the hotel lobby and logged on to the WiFi. He emailed the pictures from his phone to himself. Then to ensure the evidence was preserved, he emailed the photos and a detailed description of what he'd seen to Nigel and Harper. He looked out the windows at the pool, the lights that lined its edges and the palm tress lit by spotlights recessed in the ground. He opened his personal email.

Uncle Lane,

Don't let Christine know that I told you and don't allow this to ruin your trip.

Christine and Indiana have moved back into the house. She and Dan had a fight. She arrived last night. She says that she is going to change her name back to Lane. She said, "What Lola did was horrible, and I don't want to be associated with Dan's family anymore." She said something about living in the condominium was costing too much. Lola seemed to think because they were living there that she had control over their lives. Christine thinks there isn't much difference between being under the bishop's thumb in Paradise and being under Lola's control in the condo. She said that she was stupid for allowing someone like that into her life again.

I thought you would want to know what was going on. Now that you know, don't let it ruin your holiday. Sam is fine. He keeps looking at the door and expecting you and Arthur to arrive. Indiana and Sam are acting like old friends. Indy crawls up to Sam and the dog licks his face. Then Indiana laughs and laughs. That kid has the best laugh.

Enjoy the beach. I'll take care of Christine and Indiana. Dan will probably show up here in a day or two. How come some people think it's okay to mess with other people's lives?

Matt

Lane went for a walk by the pool, then back to the bar for a coffee in the silver urn set up for the nocturnal guests. All the time he was thinking about how to reply to his nephew.

Matt,

Thank you for letting me know what is happening.

I think Christine and I need to learn that we cannot permit others to affect us in such negative ways.

This is my fault as much as anyone's because I allowed myself to be manipulated by Lola. Thank you for taking care of things while we are away. I hope Dan will come and talk with Christine sooner rather than later. This must be difficult for him. He is caught between his loyalty to his mother and his loyalty to Christine and Indiana.

Be sure to take care of yourself. Are you and Christine still going to class?

Love,

Uncle Lane

× 53

He logged off and went back to the room where he plugged in his laptop and phone. Arthur lay in the same position as before and continued to snore. Lane decided to try to get some rest. He lay in the interminable darkness waiting for impossible sleep. The edges of the curtains gradually revealed a rising sun. He got up, retrieved his shorts and shirt, added his ball cap, sunglasses and sunscreen on his feet, and went for a walk along the beach.

The sand nearest the hotel was deep but along the edge of the ocean the footing was firm. Waves pounded the shoreline. He walked east toward the rising sun and Estero San José, a wildlife sanctuary. As the waves crashed then ran up to the beach, the sparkle of precious gems was momentarily left behind in the glare of the sun. Ahead half a dozen boarders were already swimming out to meet the rolling water. They rose up over the incoming waves and swam further out. A promising wave arrived. They turned and began to kick. The wave lifted them, and they slid down its green face. Then the wave curled over their heads and they were engulfed. Their friends on the beach erupted with coyote laughter when the surfers' heads appeared.

Lane looked ahead and saw two riders on horseback approaching. The male wore a straw hat, lifted his right hand to the brim and looked out onto the ocean. Lane turned as he heard the sound of a powerful boat. The surfers turned as well.

The cigarette boat pounded the swells. Its roar was audible over the crash of waves. Beyond the boat a whale spouted a vapour plume. Another rose more than halfway out of the water, leaned sideways and created a splash of white against the deeper blue.

The cigarette boat aimed for the whales. All of the surf-ers turned to watch. The boat drew closer to the whales. Humpback tails slapped the ocean's back as they dove. There were flashes of gunfire from the cigarette boat. The sound reached Lane seconds later.

The man on the horse said, "*Fuentes. No pinches con tu madre o tu madre pinche contigo.*"

The young woman next to him said, "Papa!"

The surfers looked up at the man, their mouths open wide. None of them made eye contact with Lane.

I think he said something about not messing with your mother or she'll mess you up. Lane turned, walked down the beach, up the stairs to the patio, past the pool and into his room. The shower was running. He stripped off his clothes, joined Arthur and thought about how to break the news of the early-morning murder.

Later, he unplugged his laptop and phone. The laptop went in the safe. He opened the phone and confirmed the pictures were still there. There were text messages from Harper and Nigel. Nigel's said, *No identity yet on the victim.* Harper's said, *Look for Alejandro.*

Arthur rubbed the top of his head with a towel. "What's it say?"

Lane recognized the curiosity in those brown eyes. *I guess this is how I'll break the news.* He handed the phone over.

Arthur looked up from the pictures. "Why didn't you wake me?"

You should see the shock on your face, Arthur. This is the nasty side of the work I do. I've tried to keep it away from you.

Arthur handed the phone back. "Don't try to protect me. I'm stronger than you think. We need to get dressed and see what's happening now." He reached into the closet for a shirt.

They walked along the corridor to the playground. The air was thick with the catch-at-the-back-of-the-throat stink of bleach. They stopped to look through the half-moon portal. PROHIBIDO EL PASO was written in black on the yellow tape wrapped around the wooden stakes and enclosing the perimeter of the wading pool fed from the whale's mouth. A quartet of workers dressed in grey and wearing blue surgical masks worked around the sculptured whale.

Lane and Arthur took the elevator to the lobby and ordered two cappuccinos from Lucy. They sat under the flat-screen TV where a soccer game played. Arthur put his sunglasses on the table. "You're back."

Lane frowned and looked at Arthur's knowing brown eyes. *What are you getting at?*

"You're back to being the person you were before the shooting."

"Christine and Matt have been writing emails and I've been writing back. I think I'm beginning to understand what happened." Lane nodded as Lucy set two tall cappuccino glasses in front of them.

Arthur handed her two US dollars. "*Gracias.*" He added a packet of raw sugar to the coffee, sipped and put the cup down on the table. "You were saying?"

"All that's happened has brought a bit of clarity. This is what it's like when the killers are free to go about their business without fear of someone like me hunting them down."

Arthur shook his head. "It wasn't obvious before?"

"Not to me."

"It was obvious to the rest of us." Arthur took another sip of coffee.

"You're going to rub my nose in it?"

Arthur set his cup down. "A little."

Lane looked at a gathering of tourists at the reception desk. "I've been that much of a pain in the ass?"

Arthur nodded. "You shut us all out. Christine took it the hardest, of course, because she's the most sensitive. Matt did his best to hold things together because that's what he does."

"And you?"

"I've been waiting for you to come back to us." Arthur lifted his coffee and sipped.

×

The late afternoon sun baked the backs of their necks, the sides of their faces and their calves between their socks and the hems of their shorts. Lane had made sure to slather his sunburnt feet with aloe vera before leaving. They walked around the southeast corner of the whitewashed concrete cemetery wall. The gates of the cemetery were chained shut. A cross was sculpted portal-like into the wall beside the ornate black iron gates.

The concrete sidewalk between the cemetery and the road was mined with manure. Two horseback riders approached. Lane and Arthur stepped to one side. There was the scent of horse, the *schnick schnick* of the leather tack, a raspberry from the horse and a nod from the rider, whom Lane recognized. *That's the guy who warned Fuentes not to mess with the sea.*

"Beautiful animals," Arthur remarked as they walked to San José, its church and the weekly evening gathering of artists.

A silver Ford pickup passed them, braked, pulled next to the curb, stopped and idled. The tropical air intensified the stink of differential fluid, grease and partially digested petroleum. The Ford's paint was mottled with what looked like salt stains. The passenger window was open. As Lane and Arthur walked past, Lane half expected to find a weapon pointed their way. Instead he saw a thirty-something driver with a thick head of black hair and a greying goatee. The driver leaned right and smiled, then asked, "Señor Lane and Señor Arthur? *Me llamo* — my name is Alejandro."

Lane stopped and took a closer look at the man who relaxed with both forearms embracing the steering wheel. He wore faded jeans and a black T-shirt with a few tattered white letters visible on this side.

Alejandro said, "A mutual acquaintance said to look out for the two of you. He called me a back-up plan."

Lane heard a mixture of American, Mexican and Canadian accents in Alejandro's English. Still, after what he'd seen this morning, Lane was reluctant.

"Everybody knows about the murder of Celia Sanchez." Alejandro lifted his eyebrows so they were visible above the frames of his Ray-Bans.

Arthur took Lane's elbow and they began to move toward San José. They ducked under the mauve blossoms of a jacaranda tree. Fifty metres further along, Alejandro's truck pulled up and stopped. Alejandro climbed out of the truck, rattle-slammed the door, walked up to Lane, handed him a cell phone, crossed his arms and waited with his feet shoulder-width apart.

"Paul, it's me."

I think this may be the second time Cam has called me Paul. "Who is this Alejandro person?"

"He's one of ours. Keely Saliba recommends him. So do I. Do you want to confirm with her as well?" Cam sounded amused but also a bit sarcastic.

You want frank? Well, then, here we go. "It's fucked-up down here. Do you have an identity on the young woman murdered this morning?"

Harper said, "Celia Sanchez. Former mistress of Ignacio Fuentes. Apparently his wife said it was over and Celia didn't believe it."

Lane nodded at Alejandro. *That confirms your story.* "The entire fucking murder has been sanitized. I saw a couple of guys haul the body away last night. A crew cleaned up the blood and shit this morning. I bet people are beginning to wonder if she ever really existed."

"What did you expect?" Cam's blunt tone added weight to his words.

Lane felt the old rage in his belly. "Don't you fuck with me!"

Cam began to laugh. Lane looked at Arthur, who was smiling. Then Lane turned to Alejandro, who was stone faced.

The sweet stink of sewage and diesel fumes hung in the air. Lane tried not to inhale.

Cam coughed. "Good to have you back. Being around you for the last few months was like eating pabulum in a Vietnamese restaurant. Bland when I'm expecting some spice. Either San José is agreeing with you or you want to get on the next plane home."

Lane shook his head and cocked his arm to throw the phone onto the roadway to be run over by a bus or one of those vans doubling as a taxi. A black open-track pace car rattled by, *Rock Star* written across the side. The passenger smiled and cupped his hands, ready to catch the phone.

"Señor?" Alejandro asked.

"What?"

Alejandro was leaning his backside against the front fender of the Ford. "Phones are very expensive here." He pulled his glasses down onto the tip of his nose so Lane could see his eyes. They were green and intelligent.

"Lane?" Harper asked.

Lane put the phone to his ear. "What!?"

"Alejandro's on your side."

"From where I stand it looks like everyone is on the side of money and guns. Fuentes makes his own laws here."

"Maybe right now he does."

"What the hell does that mean?"

"It means that the tourism industry makes more money for Mexico than the drug trade does. Change is coming to Mexico. We need to work with Alejandro so that those changes will make our streets safer as well."

Lane opened his mouth to say something, then thought better of it.

Harper said, "For once I want to take care of the supply side and the distribution side at the same time. I'm tired of putting Band-Aids on the gang problem at our end. There is a willingness on the Mexican side to shut down the suppliers. If we shut down the distribution side, then we can shut off some of the money. The gangs won't play if there's no money in it for them. They're capitalists at heart. I just need someone to tell me which players are at the table down there."

"What makes you think I should trust Alejandro?" Lane looked at the man lounging against the truck. Alejandro shrugged his shoulders and looked away.

"Years ago, Fuentes killed Alejandro's mother and sister. He wants El Guapo more than we do."

The roar of a fast-approaching vehicle made Lane look left. A pair of white Suburbans blasted past with a roar of V8 power.

Alejandro looked left over his shoulder. "Fuentes and his crowd are on the way to the art show. Are we going or not?"

"I've got to go." Lane pressed END on the phone and handed it to Alejandro. Then he reached for the passenger-side door handle. "Let's do this."

Alejandro stood up straight, walked around to the front of the truck and climbed in behind the wheel. Lane opened the passenger door and climbed in; Arthur followed. The cab smelled of tobacco, sand and grease. The floor was cluttered with empty water bottles. Arthur slammed the door, Alejandro shifted into first, the clutch shuddered and the transmission whined. Lane looked at the odometer. It was broken, as was the speedometer. It flipped over to sixty, then flopped back below zero.

They travelled in silence for about two kilometres before Arthur asked, "What's the plan?"

Alejandro leaned forward and glanced at Arthur. "We watch Fuentes and his gang, see who they talk with, especially the people who talk quietly. This way we get the lay of the land."

Lane watched the traffic just in case Alejandro was too busy talking to notice. *The way the drivers weave in and out, it's chaotic.*

Arthur asked, "Aren't you afraid of being labelled a *maricón* if you're seen with us?"

Alejandro nodded, slapped the wheel and smiled. "Being a maricón will help me become even more invisible." He slowed for a major intersection where traffic seemed to come from all directions. He crossed the road ahead of a bus that came close to clipping their rear bumper. Then he found a place to park out front of one of the shops selling cigars, tequila and Viagra. Alejandro looked at Lane and Arthur. The Latino lifted his chin and looked to the right. Lane looked ahead to where the pair of Suburbans was parked in front of the courtyard. A bodyguard dressed in black pants, black shirt and a jacket tapped his hair, which was slicked back over the top and over the collar. "I will walk one side of the street and you will walk the other. Just watch me. We cover each other's backs, agreed?"

"Okay." Lane followed Arthur out the door and onto the sidewalk. Alejandro put his sunglasses on his head and crossed the street. By the time they reached the cathedral steps, the streetlights were blinking themselves awake.

They walked past the open doors of the cathedral, then down a street with narrow sidewalks. Bright shops were adorned with colourful plates, blankets and mariposa beadwork. The Fuentes entourage consisted of El Guapo, his wife, their children, a nanny and three bodyguards. Police dressed in navy blue stood behind the traffic cones and nodded politely as the group passed. The police did the same for Lane as he walked along, his eyes expecting El Guapo's reflection in shop windows.

Alejandro took another ninety-degree turn. Lane and Arthur followed. The art in the shop windows changed from the usual brightly coloured pottery to earth tones and African sculptures. The language began to shift from Spanish to English.

Fuentes walked up the cobbled street and entered a gallery called La Hortencia. Lane turned to look into a shop across the street, then stepped inside. He looked at a polished stone sculpture inside the window. He watched one of the bodyguards, who turned his head left then right to keep an eye on approaching traffic. The man pulled a handkerchief out of his coat pocket, revealing the handgun slung under his left arm. He bent over and wiped the surface of his cream-coloured alligator boots. Lane peered inside the shop. Fuentes was greeting a tall white-haired man wearing a blue shirt. Another man wore a black muscle shirt, revealing tattoos up and down each arm. He completed the look with a ponytail and a handlebar moustache. He approached the pair and joined in conversation.

"I'll be right back," Arthur said. He left the shop, crossed the street, climbed the steps and walked past the bodyguard, who dismissed him with a glance. Moving deeper inside, Arthur accepted a proffered glass of white wine and stood in front of a painting. The painting's intense reds, blues and mauves depicted an impossibly long-limbed woman on her back on a stack of mattresses. The bottom mattress hunched its spine over a fish bowl. Arthur struck up a conversation with Fuentes's wife.

Jesus, Arthur! What the hell are you doing?

An hour later they watched the white Suburbans drive away. Then they walked over to Alejandro's Ford. It groaned as they climbed in, and complained some more when Alejandro started it up and drove back the way they had come.

"Where are we going?" Arthur asked.

Alejandro said, "You need to see something." They drove about three kilometres, passing tour buses and taxis. They turned and followed a road up the hill and parked in front of a restaurant called A la Mar in Cabo. Alejandro got out. Lane and Arthur followed. The man at the front door nodded at Alejandro but studied Lane and Arthur before gesturing them inside. Alejandro went to the right side of the restaurant, up a flight of stairs as steep as it was narrow to a room with a bar and a balcony open to the city. The waiter waved Alejandro over and sat them at a table topped with ceramic tiles.

Lane looked at Alejandro, who said, "My friends run this restaurant and have the best seafood and cold drinks. The wine comes from Mexico and so does the tequila. It's all good."

"What you like, amigos?" the waiter asked.

They made their orders. After the waiter left, Alejandro asked, "Who was that guy with the tattoos and ponytail?"

Lane said, "Manny Posadowski."

"From?"

"Calgary. He is high up in the Angels." Lane watched Alejandro gazing at the lights of Cabo San Lucas.

Arthur asked, "Who was the guy Manny and Fuentes were talking with?"

Alejandro nodded. "Luis Bonner. He lives at Palmilla."

He nodded in the other direction toward a hill rising at the tip of a peninsula. The lights of the houses rose like steps all the way to the top of Palmilla.

"We're missing some pieces," Lane said.

The waiter brought their drinks. A margarita for Lane. White wine for Arthur and red for Alejandro.

"Which ones?" Alejandro sipped the wine. A brief smile flashed in his eyes.

Lane closed his eyes when the brain freeze from the blended margarita hit him. *I've never tasted tequila like this. It's smoother than Scotch, and the limes have such intense flavour. They must grow them out back. This is potent and delicious.*

Arthur and Alejandro waited.

Lane opened his eyes. "Manny handles distribution and sales back home." He tapped his chest with an open palm. "Fuentes takes care of production."

"Bonner is the banker. He lives here in the winter and during the summer has a mansion in La Jolla, California." Alejandro pointed at Palmilla. "Some of the wealthiest people in the world have houses on Palmilla."

"And La Jolla." Arthur lifted his wine glass. "This is delicious, by the way."

"Alex is cooking us grouper. It was caught earlier today. The wine will go perfectly with the fish." Alejandro raised his glass. "You are in for a rare treat, my friends."

"Who handles the transportation from here to the States and into Canada?" Lane asked as he took a slow sip of margarita.

"He is the missing fresa. They call him Keystone." Alejandro stared at his wine glass.

"What exactly is a fresa? A tourist, maybe?" Arthur asked.

Alejandro stared at his wine. "Strawberry. It's our word for someone who is rich, white and arrogant."

"Keystone?" Lane asked.

"A nickname for the drug pipeline."

I recognize that look in Alejandro's eyes. He isn't seeing red wine; he's seeing blood. Lane sat back and looked at the lights on Palmilla. "Who owns the house at the top of the hill?"

Alejandro smiled. "Bonner."

Feeling a little light-headed, Lane locked the nail of his right forefinger behind his thumbnail, held it up, closed his right eye and flicked his middle finger at Bonner's house.

Arthur asked, "What the hell are you doing?"

"Imagining knocking Bonner off his perch."

chapter 10

Uncle Lane,

It was good to see you and Indiana together the other night. I knew that he was missing you. He slept so well that night.

I've been thinking about what you said about not letting Lola affect us. As far as I can tell that's very easy to say. She's Dan's mother. She's Indiana's grandmother. Dan's sister Linda moved away right after high school to get away from her. And if my mother's any indication of a person's inability to change, Lola will always be like this. With the damage she's done to Linda, Dan and you, I think it will be better if Indiana grows up away from all of that. It took me a long time to even think about forgiving my mother. To tell the truth, I may never forgive her totally. And what Lola did to you was so cold and calculated. Indiana needs to be protected from people like her. People like that do damage so callously and use all kinds of excuses to rationalize their abuse when it's really about getting what they want.

By now Matt will have told you that Indy and I have moved back into the house. Just don't let him know that I know. I'm also considering changing my name back to Lane.

Don't worry about Indy and me. Matt and Sam are taking good care of us. And yes, I'm still going to class.

Love,

Christine

Uncle Lane,

We're doing just fine here. Sam is watching over Indy as if he senses that the little guy needs to be protected.

Christine is still very angry about what happened and is determined to protect Indy from the kind of abuse she experienced as a child. I can't really blame her for that.

The funny thing is that the families we were born into gave us an appreciation for the kind of family you and Uncle Arthur created.

We're doing fine. Hope you and Uncle Arthur are enjoying a quiet and restful vacation. Have you seen any whales yet?

Matt

×

Lane sat out on their pool level patio drinking a coffee he'd carried down from the lobby. He thought about Christine, Indy, Matt and Dan. He thought about what he'd learned last night about the drug operation and what it would take to dismantle a cartel.

"In every culture in the history of the world people drink beer because they like beer!" The male voice carried across the pool, then echoed back from the walls of the resort. Thankfully, for a moment at least, the drunk's volume was washed away by the sound of a wave crashing against the shoreline. Lane pulled out his phone and checked the time: eight thirty. He leaned left and spotted a black-bearded thirty-something man in the pool. He wore a white ball cap. His hat, head, shoulders and cerveza were visible above the water. He spoke at two women wrapped in towels, sitting on a pair of blue lounge chairs.

"Beer is the most important fermented drink in history. It served as a water purifier in many societies!" He raised his bottle to the sun as if to illustrate his point.

A girl of five or six ran along the edge of the pool. She wore a pink dress and a tiara.

"HEY, KID!" The drunk waved at the child.

The girl stopped and looked down at the man.

"Tell them —" the drunk pointed at the women in the lounge chairs "— that beer tastes better than all other fermented drinks."

"No," the girl said.

"Why not?" the drunk's voice boomed. "Don't you like beer?"

"No. My grandma says it tastes like horse piss." The girl ran along the edge of the pool and through a doorway.

Lane smiled at the momentary quiet. *This guy must have been drinking all night.*

The drunk stood up so the water was just under his navel. "That princess doesn't know what she's talking about!"

Thirty seconds later two men appeared. Lane noted the anger written up and down their spines. Both were nearly six feet tall. Each weighed over two hundred pounds. One appeared to be sixty; the other, half that. Both had beards, one white and one red. They stood at the edge of the pool facing the drunk.

Lane got up from his chair, stepped carefully around a bougainvillea and onto the sidewalk. *This could turn nasty really quickly.*

The older man said, "You scared my granddaughter."

The drunk began to back up. "I was just asking her if she likes beer, man!"

"Then why is she crying?" Red Beard asked.

The drunk raised his arms. "I'm a Canadian! I'm peaceful. I come from Fort Mac!"

Grey Hair pointed at himself and red beard. "We're Canadian. My granddaughter is Canadian."

"Is there a problem, señor?" The security guard wore a white shirt, black pants and black ball cap. He was shorter than either of the bearded men, yet he inserted himself neatly between them and the man in the pool.

"I just asked the princess if she liked beer!" The drunk stood up and held out crucified-cerveza arms.

The security guard turned to White Beard. "How old is your granddaughter, amigo?"

White Beard kept his eyes on the drunk. "Five."

"She was wearing a pink dress?" the security guard asked. Red Beard nodded.

"My name is Felix." The security guard put his hand to his chest. "Your granddaughter, her name is Ella?"

Lane stepped forward. "I saw what happened." Lane pointed at the drunk. "That one frightened Ella." White Beard's eyes lasered into the drunk.

The security guard eyed Lane as another complication.

One of the women on the blue deck chair said, "He's harmless. He just needs to sleep it off."

If he's so harmless, why is Ella crying? Lane looked at the woman who wore sunglasses. Beside her were five empty glasses: one upright, four on their sides.

Another security guard arrived, this one taller than anyone else.

The drunk began to lean to one side. His reflexes were off. He stumbled, then slipped underwater in slow motion. He momentarily managed to keep his beer above periscope depth; then the bottle went under.

The guards and the beards waited. The drunk came up once, vomited and went back down.

The guards jumped in and dragged him to the side of the pool. Lane grabbed the sleeves of the drunk's T-shirt, then pulled his dead-seal weight onto the deck, dodging another rush of vomit.

By the time the cleaning crew arrived, the pool had been shut down, more sun worshippers and swimmers had arrived to reserve deck chairs and the drunk had been carted off to his room in a wheelchair. As Lane walked back to his room, he spotted a toupee atop the purple flowers of the bougainvillea hedge. By breakfast word had spread that the asshole drunk who puked in the pool and closed it down was named Dixon.

Frederick listened to Mrs. Baker saying, "Arthur Miller stripped away the layers of the American Dream to expose its reality." He gently flexed his shoulder. The swelling was down this morning, and Tylenol was taking care of most the pain. Each pellet wound had a colourful bruise. He was careful to disguise the pain he felt so no one would suspect he was recovering from a gunshot wound. That's why it was so important to be at school. The first few days were crucial so he could not be connected to the shooting. The papers were full of the story. The police were saying some evidence had been recovered from the car and they were searching for a suspect who drove a stolen red Mustang. He hoped the recovered evidence wasn't blood. DNA would be difficult to explain away. Mrs. Baker continued: "Willie lives a delusion. A delusion that success is only attributable to personal attractiveness and money."

Frederick looked at his fingernails and wondered whether it was time for a manicure.

×

Christine, Matt, Dan and Indiana,

Arthur and I have been thinking that perhaps we would like to have another holiday in the sun. This place is very nice.

We were hoping we could vacation together here. You know, everyone gets a room, has some sun in the wintertime, takes time to relax and decompress. There may be an opportunity for us to purchase some time down here.

What do you think?

Love,

Lane and Arthur

×

Arthur tapped Lane on the knee as they sat in the lobby. Lane pressed SEND, then logged off. He looked up.

Alejandro wore a loose white linen shirt and khaki shorts. His cheeks were shaved and his hair was slicked straight back. His green eyes were hidden behind Ray-Bans. *He's a chameleon*, Lane thought. *Even his walk is different.* Today he adopted a cocky confidence exuding wealth. Single women sitting at nearby lobby tables turned to watch him as he strode by.

Alejandro pulled out a chair and sat down with Lane and Arthur. Lane saw the shoulders of one or two hopeful women sag. One blonde who'd been hydrating with rum said, "All the good-looking ones are gay."

"You want a coffee?" Lane asked.

Alejandro nodded. "Love one."

Arthur said, "Who are you today?"

Alejandro smiled and lifted his chin. "A fresa."

"How can I be a fresa? My parents came from Lebanon."
Arthur sipped his drink.

Alejandro took off his sunglasses and set them on the table. He looked more closely at Arthur. "You're close enough to pass." He winked.

Janet, a waitress with an angelic face, walked over. "Anything else?"

Arthur held up three fingers. "Three cappuccinos, please." Janet smiled and turned. Arthur tapped Alejandro's arm. "What do I have to do to be a better fresa?"

Alejandro leaned forward. "Act like a wealthy, snobby, arrogant person who wears lots of bling and looks like this." He turned his head to the left to lift his collar and reveal his profile. "I'm living the American Dream and I own a place on Palmilla next door to a billionaire." He flashed a plastic smile. "In fact, I *am* a billionaire and I own a yacht."

Arthur smiled.

"Where are we going?" Lane asked.

"Ah, I forgot, you like to get right to the point. We are going whale watching on a great big boat with a bunch of drunk, horny tourists so that we can blend in and take a close look at Bonner's little boat."

Bonner's "little boat" was black, about forty metres long, and had a helicopter parked aft on a helipad and *Fire* crested in sparkling stainless-steel letters on its side. It was three times the size of any other vessel in the Cabo San Lucas harbour. Lane, Arthur and Alejandro got a close look at it as they leaned on the port-side railing of the lower deck of a white catamaran called *Sundancer.* Alejandro used a pair of binoculars to inspect *Fire* from stem to stern, then handed the binoculars to Lane. He looked out along the empty decks and the white-wrapped helicopter on the helipad. *How many tonnes of cocaine were sold to buy this?*

The deck of *Sundancer* began to vibrate as it eased away from the dock. Lane took a close look at the bridge of *Fire*, but there was no indication of movement behind the polarized safety glass.

Sundancer moved out into the harbour. They passed the fishing boats and a gunboat with its masked marines holding automatic weapons and a heavy machine gun mounted on a platform above their heads. On the starboard side, wrinkled, weathered sand-coloured peaks poked their noses out of the ocean. *Sundancer* slowed to pass the famous arch where the green water became choppy from the crowd of boats. Tour boats of various shapes and sizes eased in and around for a closer look. *Sundancer*'s diesel engines growled as it cut through the gentle swells.

Fifteen minutes later they were on the open sea and spotted several smaller boats gathered near a particular patch of ocean. A cloud of vapour rose into the air. A cry went up from the people sitting in lawn chairs at the bow. *Sundancer* turned, keeping its distance from the whales. Arthur pulled his camera from his pocket and leaned against the railing. Moments later the whale spouted again as its grey–blue back surfaced. A smaller whale surfaced next to it. A third whale swam beside them before arching its back and revealing the white underside of its tail. It dove deep.

Alejandro tapped Lane on the shoulder and pointed at an approaching vessel. Lane recognized its lean elongated bow and white hull even before the sound of its engines reached their ears. The cigarette boat cut a swath between the smaller boats as it bore down on the whales. Mother and calf dove. The cigarette boat roared though the flat patch left on the water's surface by the whales' dive. The smaller boats bobbed in the wake of the faster boat. It came within twenty metres of *Sundancer*. Lane noted the name *Wind* written across the boat's bow as he spotted two men standing in the cockpit. One was at the helm; the other was laughing. Lane recognized Bonner and Fuentes. Manny and another man sat behind them. The Hells Angel waved his hands as he emphasized a point. Manny was facing Lane; the other man had his back to *Sundancer* and did not look their way. The cigarette boat crested swells then splashed into troughs as it raced toward the harbour.

"Did you get a good look at the two in the back?" Lane turned to Alejandro, who followed the boat with his binoculars.

Alejandro waited a moment before he shook his head. "Just the one you call Manny."

Laughter came from the forward deck. The three of them moved toward the bow. A man lay on his back. A woman straddled him. A blue balloon squeaked in between their crotches. They worked together, simulating passion. The balloon popped and the crowd roared approval. Another couple was chosen. This time the man came at the woman from behind. Arthur moved to the stern. The other two followed.

An hour later, the *Sundancer* was on its way back to the harbour. They passed El Arco de Cabo San Lucas at sunset. The sun and thin layer of cloud created a red-and-purple backdrop to the arch. In the foreground a woman on a catamaran lifted her sleeveless top to reveal her breasts. "So that's what those look like," Arthur said dryly.

Alejandro laughed and slapped Arthur on the back. They eased up to the berth ten minutes later. The cigarette boat *Wind* was tied up alongside *Fire* and the lights were on in the cabin beneath *Fire's* helipad.

Lane followed Arthur and Alejandro as they stepped off the stern of *Sundancer*. He kept himself between the crowd and *Fire* so he could watch any goings-on.

When they arrived at a four-door Jeep, Alejandro asked, "What did you see?" Lane shook his head as he climbed in the passenger seat. Arthur got in the back.

"Mexico is all about the people you know, right?" Arthur asked.

"Of course." Alejandro turned on the key and the windows whirred down.

"Canada is like that, and so is the US. It's all about the people you know." Arthur slid over and leaned forward so his head was between Lane and Alejandro. "Did you notice the yacht?"

"What are you getting at?" Lane asked.

"It rides low in the water. They must be setting up a transportation system. The cigarette boat carries the cargo to the yacht. The yacht carries the cargo north. They have contacts in the north who transfer the cargo at sea and then the cargo gets to the mainland and ultimately to its customers." Arthur looked at each of them in turn. "It's right in front of our faces. The marinas are either unaware or are being paid to look the other way."

Alejandro nodded. "Bonner, Fuentes, Manny and Keystone all have their contacts along the way. So we're looking at what you would call a hub?"

"Right under our noses." Lane smiled at Arthur.

"It's so obvious that it's almost invisible!" Arthur sat back. "Now let's go have dinner and a margarita!"

"I know a place." Alejandro started the engine and drove them back along the highway, past the entrance to Palmilla, then to the restaurant of his friend, where today's catch of lobster and shrimp was waiting.

×

Lane checked his email when they got back to the hotel.

Uncle Lane,

Don't bullshit us. We know you're on the job. Cam and Erinn Harper have phoned at least four times to ask how we're doing. Marked and unmarked units drive by at least every ten minutes. We feel very, very safe.

Matt thinks your being in Cabo San Lucas has something to do with the gang war that's erupting in Calgary. I saw on Facebook that gang suppression officers are hitting restaurants and bars. The media is speculating that we are about to become like Vancouver, Toronto or Montreal. They say the gang violence is getting out of hand.

I don't know exactly why you are there, but you'd both better come home safe.

Love,

Christine and Indiana

He thought for a few minutes, sipped a soda water, then began to type a reply.

Christine, Indiana, Dan and Matt,

All right. Busted.

We went to Cabo San Lucas today, saw some whales, had a great meal and got some work done. That's about all I can say right now.

Hope everyone is doing well there. We miss you and hope to see you soon. Could we go out for dinner when we get back?

Love,

Uncle Lane

He sent the message, then composed a second email.

Cam and Nigel,

Thank you for keeping an eye on my family while we are here. Arthur offered an interesting theory while we were in Cabo San Lucas today. A yacht named Fire is berthed in the harbour. A cigarette boat is tied up alongside. Arthur thinks that Luis Bonner, Manny Posadowski and Ignacio Fuentes are setting up a transportation system. The cigarette boat transports the cargo from the mainland to Cabo San Lucas and offloads it onto the yacht. The yacht sails north and offloads the drugs to be transported from there. The fourth member of their team (we've nicknamed him Keystone) is yet to be identified. We did spot a fourth suspect in the cigarette boat today but were unable to make a positive ID.

It's likely that various key contacts here, in San Diego and perhaps in Vancouver or Nanaimo assist in transferring cargo from the yacht to the mainland.

Do you have eyes on members of Moreau's former transportation network? There may be someone (Keystone?) from Moreau's old gang at that end who is about to make use of them to transport cargo from Nanaimo/Vancouver, across the Rockies and into our neck of the woods.

Lane

chapter 11

CC. Nigel Li

Lane,

Nigel and I have put our heads together, connected with some of his contacts and mine to see what members of Moreau's old network are up to. One of our gang suppression team members has noticed interactions between one of Moreau's cousins and one of Manny's lieutenants.

If possible, get a positive ID on Keystone.

We continue to track the driver of the second vehicle (the Mustang) involved in the shooting on Stoney Trail. A handgun was found tucked down beside the driver's seat. It is a Beretta like the weapon left at the Sleeping Dragon restaurant shooting. The forensics unit found evidence confirming two tires were shot out in the truck by the second recovered Beretta. Dr. Weaver also found blood evidence in the Mustang. The two fatalities were in the truck. Both have been identified as FOB members. Nigel is tracking two persons of interest to see if he can identify the shooter.

Cam

×

Lane ate a breakfast of fresh pineapple, yogurt, crisp bacon and an omelette filled with tomatoes, peas and corn. He and Arthur sat at a table on the patio as waves rushed in and crashed onto the beach. A wave curled and the wind blew white water back. For a moment it reminded Lane of horses charging the beach. He reached for his coffee. "How about we take a walk on the beach after breakfast?"

Arthur smiled. "You sure we can take a break from our jobs?"

Twenty minutes later, they walked out onto the sand where men and women in white tops, pants and hats waited with cigars, suitcases of silver jewellery, stacks of hats and collections of colourful scarves for sale. One asked, "Señor?"

Arthur said, "*No gracias.*"

A man in a wide-brimmed straw hat asked, "Cuban cigars, amigo?"

"*No gracias,*" Lane said.

With heads down, they slogged though the soft sand on the way to the edge of the ocean.

The man followed. "Want ganja?"

Arthur shook his head and continued to walk away.

"Cocaína?" the man continued. "Good stuff."

"Did he say kokanee?" Arthur asked.

Lane shook his head as they reached the firmer sand close to the water.

A boy and a girl rode horseback toward them. A man in a wide-brimmed hat followed. The boy might have been ten, the girl a year or two older. Her shoulder-length hair was blown back. A wave ran up the beach and up the horse's knees. The boy began to laugh. The girl joined in. There was something pure and wild in their voices. It stopped Lane. The wave rolled up over his shoes and too late he danced onto dry sand.

Arthur laughed and put his hand on Lane's shoulder. "Those kids were having so much fun. When was the last time we laughed like that?"

✕

Alejandro was waiting for them at the red-roofed beach bar when they got back from their walk. He sipped from a water bottle and pointed out at the sea. "Whales."

Lane and Arthur turned to watch. About a minute later the grey–blue back of a whale surfaced. A moment later, a smaller one appeared.

"The baby," Alejandro said as one of the adult whales launched itself out of the water. It reached for the sky then fell sideways into the ocean in a mountain of white.

"Amazing!" Arthur said.

They watched in silence for five minutes. Whales surfaced, spouted and every so often rose up to touch the horizon. Then they were gone.

"We're going back to our room. Lane needs to change his shoes." Arthur pointed at his partner's feet.

"Waves will sneak up on you." Alejandro smiled and followed them along the curving path leading to their room.

Alejandro sat on the patio and sipped his water while Lane and Arthur got ready.

Lane joined Alejandro on the patio. Alejandro looked across the pool. Fuentes sat on a blue lounge chair and watched as his children swam. His wife sat next to him holding their youngest child, who was asleep, wrapped in a gold towel.

"It all looks so ordinary. Parents caring for their children and relaxing by the pool," Alejandro said.

Lane nodded.

"You have a family?" Alejandro sipped his water and looked right at the ocean.

"A nephew and a niece and her son and husband." Lane frowned.

"There's a problem?"

"Our niece moved back into our house without her husband."

Alejandro nodded. "He is not good for her?"

"He's very nice. His mother is a ..." *What do I call Lola, exactly?*

"A fresa?"

"A very good word for Lola!"

"This Lola, she is a showgirl?" Alejandro winked.

Lane laughed.

Arthur stepped out onto the deck. "What's so funny?" Lane told him. Arthur smiled. "Yes, come to think of it, she is a showgirl." He looked at Lane. "Lola tried to get our niece to put on white makeup before introducing Christine to her country club friends."

"Your niece has dark skin?" Alejandro lifted an eyebrow and a brown arm.

"She's —" Arthur looked at Lane before continuing " — biracial."

Alejandro shook his head. "I can't understand why it makes a difference."

Arthur put his hand on Lane's shoulder. "Lola told Paul that she didn't want him around our grandson Indiana after Paul had to shoot a killer."

Alejandro scratched his head and looked at Lane.

Arthur continued. "He killed a murderer and arrested his wife. They were a team. They travelled around robbing and killing people. The man was about to shoot a boy."

"I read about this. They killed a couple in Cancun and another in New York?" Alejandro squeezed his plastic water bottle and it crackled.

Lane nodded.

"And this Lola, she went for your, how do you say, *huevos?*"

"Huevos?" Lane asked.

"Eggs." Alejandro mimicked grabbing his crotch.

"Balls," Arthur said.

"That's right. Some people are like that. They try to take your strength away." Alejandro looked across the pool at Fuentes and his family. "They think that they can take from others without consequence to themselves. They are usually rich and powerful and believe that they cannot be touched."

They looked at the pool and watched Fuentes as he pointed at his son who was splashing water in his sister's face.

"What was taken from you?" Arthur asked.

"My mother and sister. I was nine." The bottle crackled in Alejandro's hand. "Fuentes ran them down in the street. My little brother and I watched it happen. The police said it was an accident. My father was working in Canada at the time. He moved us there after the funeral."

"And he —" Lane cocked his head in the direction of Fuentes "— brought you back?"

"In a way, yes. We have different natures, he and I. I want him to face the consequences of his actions. He thinks he is immune from them." Alejandro stood up. "We have some work to do before that will happen, amigos. Are you coming?"

"Where?" Arthur opened the sliding glass door and stepped back into the room.

"Manny and his boys have a place just inland from here." Alejandro followed Arthur inside. Lane locked the sliding door then the door to the room. They walked along the hallway, past the children's playground, upstairs to the lobby and outside. Alejandro had a white Chrysler 300 parked out on the street. They climbed inside, Alejandro started up and they drove toward San José. He turned left at the cemetery and travelled a kilometre north. A man in a white hat, shirt and pants sat against the white wall at the entrance to a clutch of white condominiums. Beside the man was a metre-high wall engraved with the image of a whale. Lane looked at the man, the way his body sagged and his arms hung at his side.

Alejandro said, "Manny and his boys have a couple of condos there. The ones where the Harleys are parked."

"Do you have any contacts with the local police?" Lane asked.

"Yes." Alejandro looked sideways at Lane. "Why?"

"That man propped up against the wall is dead. The bikers are sending a message. It may be the man who tried to sell us cocaine this morning. Manny and the boys are marking their territory." Lane took a long breath. *Like dogs pissing on each other's scent.*

Arthur turned to look at the body. "How can you tell?"

Lane shrugged. *Believe me, I can tell.*

Alejandro's phone rang thirty minutes later as they sat drinking coffee under an umbrella on the patio out front of a San José restaurant called Pete's. "*Hola?*"

Lane and Arthur listened to the rapid-fire Spanish.

Alejandro pressed END on the phone, put it on the table and pointed his index finger to his temple. "One bullet in the side of the head. Close range. These guys think that no one can touch them."

"Not for much longer," Arthur said.

I wish I shared your optimism.

That evening, as the sun stretched long fingers of lazy light across the resort, Lane sat on the patio waiting for Arthur to get ready. They had a six o'clock reservation for dinner.

The noise of automatic gunfire carried over the water but was drowned when a wave crashed on the beach.

chapter 12

In the morning the staff was usually smiling with friendly *holas*. But this morning, as Lane and Arthur walked around the pool to the breakfast buffet, there was worry and an undercurrent of what Lane took to be anger. An unpleasant smell rose from the beach. As Carlos poured their coffee, Lane saw people gathering near the water. A grey–blue shape lay on the beach, rocking in the waves. A larger wave curled over the body and splashed down on its back. Blood oozed from a series of puncture wounds above its eye. The wounds reached halfway along its back. "Is that the whale calf?" Arthur asked.

Lane nodded as three quads buzzed up the beach. The manager of La Luna Cortez looked first at the whale's corpse then out at the ocean where a pair of whales swam and spouted. They were abnormally close, just beyond where the waves began to gather on their gallop to the beach.

A man arrived riding a horse and trailing three others linked by a rope. He wore a straw hat, a long-sleeved shirt and washed-out jeans. He leaned over and talked to the manager, who was shading his eyes with his right hand. They talked for a few minutes; then the rider nudged his horse's ribs with his heels and continued along the beach. The manager looked back at the resort and frowned.

Arthur said, "It was the guys in the cigarette boat, wasn't it?"

Lane nodded. "I think so." *So many people here rely on the tourists for their families. Manny, Bonner, Fuentes and Keystone are not making themselves popular with the locals.*

The stench intensified as the sun baked the carcass. Lane stood up, leaving his coffee unfinished. "I'm going up to the lobby to use the WiFi."

Arthur looked toward their room. "I'm going to get changed, then come back to keep an eye on the beach. Come and get me when you're done."

Lane followed Arthur to the room, picked up his laptop and phone, then went out and along the hallway. He looked left through the portal at the whale's mouth where he'd seen Celia Sanchez's body. He walked past the entrance to the children's play area. Brown-haired twin girls of seven or eight looked up at their father as they waited for him to open the door. The smell of bleach lingered in the air and became more intense when the father opened the door. Lane continued on to the stairway and made his way up to the lobby. He sat down, opened his laptop and checked his email.

Uncle Lane,

Hope you are finding time to enjoy the sun and the beach. Sam is on the rug beside me as I write this. Christine and Indiana are sleeping.

Dan came over today to see Indiana and Christine. I left them alone to talk and took Sam for a walk. Dan was gone when I got back, and Christine was putting Indy to sleep. I don't know exactly what is going on, but I hope they can work it out.

When do you and Arthur get back?

Matt

Lane began to type.

Matt,

Thanks for letting me know what's going on. I'm also hoping that they can figure things out. We all knew that Lola was difficult to deal with. Linda was a real eye-opener for me. She moved far away so she wouldn't have to deal with Lola. Dan, on the other hand, is the kind of person who feels loyalty toward his parents. It is his strength and weakness. As a result, he has a difficult choice to make.

We're doing well here. The place is beautiful. The food is wonderful, and Arthur is out soaking up some sun.

I don't know how much longer we will be down here. There are a few things we need to check out before returning.

Love,

Uncle Lane

Next he opened a message from Nigel.

Lane,

We're still working on the Frederick angle at Thirsk High School. Frederick Lee has a spotless record, but I watched the guy leave school on the security cameras. The other kids gave him a wide berth and no one except a high-stepping blonde girl would make eye contact with him. The other odd thing was that none of the boys nearby would even glance at the blonde. Lee drives a black Mercedes SUV with right-hand drive. There's just something about the kid that makes me think we need to watch him. You know how you tell me to trust my gut? Well, my gut is working overtime when it comes to Mr. Lee.

Hope you're getting some time in the sun down there. I know Lori is joking about you getting a tan. Better not disappoint her!

Nigel

✕

"*Pinche narcos!*" Janet, the angel-faced waitress, wore a black skirt and vest, had her black hair tied back and presented an uncharacteristic frown as she set a cappuccino on the table in front of Lane. He followed her gaze past the railing to the reservations desk where Fuentes had arrived with his entourage of family, maids and bodyguards. Two bellhops in blue hotel shirts and shorts pushed a pair of carts piled high with luggage.

"Palmilla!" Fuentes said, then threw a handful of plastic door keys at the woman behind the desk. She leaned to her left as one of the cards whipped by her ear.

The manager stepped out from a side door. He crossed his arms and watched as Fuentes led his group outside to a waiting pair of white Suburbans. Lane noticed the bellhops using exaggerated care when they loaded the baggage. Then he looked at the faces of the staff standing around the perimeter of the foyer. No one spoke. The Suburbans pulled away. The staff glanced around at the various exits as if expecting some calamity to arrive.

Frederick flexed his right shoulder. The decreased level of pain, itching and tingling told him the wounds were healing. He looked over his computer monitor as people entered and left the library. His teacher, Mr. Harvey, talked to the librarian and did not see a student with his arm up.

Frederick went over the aftermath of the shooting in his mind. His clothes were safely stashed in a garbage bin at the local daycare. It was unlikely anyone would go through bags of shitty diapers to look for evidence. The gun had been wiped clean and tucked next to the seat of the Mustang. The only thing he worried about was blood. If any was left behind from his wounded shoulder, his DNA would connect him to the car and the gun.

He closed his eyes and tried to remember whether he'd wiped away all blood spatter on the seat, then recalled the yellow, green and purple bruising he'd seen around the pellet wounds this morning. To assume there was no spatter would be a mistake. He needed a backup plan now, one involving a passport and cash.

×

Lane and Arthur sat on the deck chairs on the patio outside of their room. The tropical night was punctuated with stars. The middle of the complex was being pounded with music from a tiki party on the beach. To their left a gathering of Canadians sat near the pool. "Shit! I spilled my drink!" a deep male voice announced.

"You're such a klutz, Steve!" A woman's nasal voice was loud even over the tiki music.

"Shut up, Anita! Get me another drink!" Steve said.

Another voice, conciliatory, yet just as drunk, said, "Relax. I've got it."

"Arnie's got it!" Anita said.

Arthur got up, opened the sliding glass door and went inside; Lane followed. Arthur said, "Sounds like the drunks are auditioning for a reality show."

Lane sat on his bed, leaned a couple of pillows against the headboard, grabbed the remote and began to flip through the channels on the flat-screen TV. Arthur went into the bathroom. "Just putting some cream on my knees and elbows." The TV blinked to black as the lights went out and the whir of the air conditioning died. Lane got up and felt his way to the bathroom. The music from the tiki party had gone silent.

Arthur asked, "What happened?"

Lane looked in the direction of the door to the hallway. There was no line of light between the floor and the door. "I don't know."

Some light came in through the door to the patio. Lane felt around for the closet door, opened it, touched the safe's keypad and entered the numbers. The safe opened and he retrieved his phone and credit cards.

"What are you doing?" Arthur asked.

"We're leaving the room and going outside." Lane felt around for his sandals. "Got your shoes on?"

"Yes."

"Ready?" Lane felt Arthur's hand on his shoulder. He opened the door and looked into the hallway. The only light came from a locked glass door leading outside. He stepped into the hall, turned left and saw a solitary exterior light illuminating the pathway to the pool. They felt their way along the hall, down the steps and out onto the pathway. Lane looked left. Half the resort was in darkness. Lights illuminated the grounds and the pools. Smoke drifted from one corner of the complex. He caught a whiff of raw petroleum.

"FIRE!" A man pointed at the smoke, then at a woman on a second-floor balcony. "Anita!"

"FIRE!" Anita pointed at the moon. "STEVE!" The red tip of her cigarette was visible.

Steve pointed with a half-empty Corona. "Anita baby, are you okay?"

Anita leaned over the balcony. Her ample cleavage cut a canyon in the moonlight. "Come get me, baby!"

Steve's feet started moving. His arms and shoulders were a little slower. He leaned right and fell into the bougainvillea next to the pathway.

"*Dos cervezas!*" The voice came from the other side of the pool.

"This is better than fuckin' *Romeo and Juliet*," someone said.

Lane looked away from the bizarre balcony scene and toward the café where lights shone through the windows.

"Let's go over there."

A man in a straw hat walked along the illuminated hallway next to the café. He wore a muscle shirt to showcase his blue tattoos. He carried two fishing poles in his right hand and pulled his luggage with his left.

Lane and Arthur stood outside and watched with a few of the waiters from the café. Another man walked past. The wheels of his golf cart thumped over the tiles. His elementary-school-age son and preschool daughter followed, then his wide-eyed wife carrying her purse and a box of golf balls.

Arthur said, "He certainly has his priorities figured out."

Lane raised his eyebrows as the maître d' from one of the restaurants said, "Please, we need everyone to go to the beach!" She began to wave guests forward to where tables and chairs were being set up. Lane found a table with white seat covers and a tablecloth. He sat down. A woman sat down across from him, cradling her sleeping son in her arms. The boy's father sat down next to her. Another family, including grandmother, aunts, mothers, brothers and grandchildren, sat down. One of the children was sound asleep and stretched across two chairs. A teenaged girl began to translate from Spanish to English and back again.

About an hour later, after the staff had brought warm towels down to the beach and Arthur had run out of things to say to their tablemates, Lane got up and went for a walk. He followed the lit stairway up to the resort lobby. Firemen stood outside the front doors. Oxygen tanks and helmets lay scattered around the pillars. A police officer with an assault rifle slung over his shoulder stood leaning against a wall. Alejandro was there wearing jeans, a black T-shirt and sneakers. He stood away from the crowd and talked on his phone unnoticed among the hotel staff and various emergency workers. He looked up and nodded at Lane, then cocked his head in the direction of the karaoke bar. Lane went outside and saw fire engines and ambulances parked around the fountain. More firemen, police and resort security gathered here and there. He walked back through the sliding glass doors and downstairs to the sunken karaoke bar. Alejandro sat in a chair with his back against the wall. Lane sat down next to him.

"Arthur is fine?"

Lane nodded. "They have us down on the beach. The staff is taking good care of us, passing around sandwiches, warm towels and coffee."

"The hotel staff will tell you that the fire was electrical. An accident. One of my friends is a fireman. He says that there was a strong smell of kerosene where the fire originated in the laundry. He thinks someone set fire to a load of towels in a dryer. It's next to the elevator and the fuse boxes for one side of the building. So the hotel's calling it an electrical fire and my friend is saying it was arson."

Lane nodded. "The resort manager had an argument with Fuentes about a whale calf that washed up on the beach."

"Fuentes and Manny have been using the whales for target practice. People all around the harbour are talking about it. The guys who run the whale tours are worried but can't say anything to Fuentes or their houses will burn down." Alejandro looked at his reflection in the glass to make sure that no one was listening in by sitting close to the railing above.

"Fuentes was saying something about Palmilla."

Alejandro nodded. "He can certainly afford to stay at the hotel. Celebrities and billionaires do. You moving to another hotel?"

Lane shook his head. "Don't think so. We've got our role to play and this seems to be where the action is."

Alejandro nodded. "I'm not sure where we go from here."

"We use our eyes and ears."

Alejandro took his phone out of his pocket. Lane saw the frown forming in the lines across Alejandro's forehead. "Expecting a text?"

Alejandro raised his eyebrows and cocked his head to the left. "I met someone down here."

Lane saw the subtle differences in Alejandro's facial muscles and heard a softening in his tone of voice. "Hmmm."

"What?" Alejandro leaned away as if to get a clearer look at Lane.

"Your posture changed. Your eyes narrowed."

Alejandro's phone beeped. He read the text and smiled.

"It changed again."

Alejandro looked up from his phone. "What did?"

"Your eyes. Your face. Your tone of voice."

"We are engaged. She works here at the resort."

"What's her name?"

"Karen."

"Your voice changes when you say her name."

"This is a science for you?" Alejandro smiled.

"What's that?"

"This reading of people's reactions."

"It is useful in my line of work. You can tell a great deal about a person by watching the eyes and listening for changes in the tone of voice."

Alejandro took a breath. "You and Arthur started a family."

"By accident. First our nephew Matt arrived on our doorstep, and then our niece Christine."

"She has the little boy?"

"Indiana."

"Your voice changes when you say their names." Alejandro lifted his eyebrows.

"You are a fast learner."

Alejandro nodded. "I want you to be very careful the next

day or so, just in case you and your Arthur are the targets and this fire is — how you say?"

"A diversion?"

"Yes, that is the word. Fuentes has been able to live this long because he has the survival instincts of a coyote."

Lane asked, "Like one of those ruthless guys who takes people across the border or like the coyotes back home that can survive anywhere?"

"I think both."

chapter 13

Lane sat in the foyer of La Luna Cortez with his laptop and a cappuccino. Men in dress shirts and ties walked back and forth. They were remarkable only because each had his black hair slicked back and wore black dress pants with a crisp white shirt. Lane watched the tourists walk by avoiding eye contact.

The man at the next table leaned in. "Timeshare salesmen. It's like their uniform: tailored shirt and pants, hair slicked back so it hangs over the collar." The man wore an orange Los Cabos T-shirt and a black ball cap with fluorescent pink hair sticking out at the top and sides. "How long you been here, man?" His boozy voice had a sports announcer's volume and echoed in the foyer.

"A few days." Lane smiled.

"Name's Vic." The man stretched out a beefy hand and shook Lane's.

Lane inhaled a disconcerting blend of mint, coconut oil and second-hand rum. "Lane." He released Vic's grip and leaned back in the chair.

They turned as a pair of Prada stilettos announced the arrival of a woman of indeterminate age wearing a chic red sleeveless A-line dress and shoulder-length, jet-black hair. Vic said, "That's the woman in charge of the cabana boys."

"Cabana boys?" *What the hell is he talking about?*

"I call the timeshare salesmen cabana boys. They'll do whatever you want as long as you end up buying a timeshare. She sits behind the one-way glass in the corner of the room, a queen bee watching over the workers. After the deal is consummated — so to speak — you're a ghost."

Lane nodded.

"Better hang onto your balls when that one's nearby. I figure she's got a collection in that office of hers. All those cabana boys are in the palm of her hand." Vic lifted a mint green mojito glass with his right hand, grabbed his crotch with his left, then took a long pull on his drink.

Arthur walked down the hallway. He wore a white shirt, khaki shorts, his Mediterranean chocolate tan and a smile as he sat down across from Lane. Lane lifted his eyebrows. *What has he gotten us into this time?*

"I've got a surprise for you." Arthur smiled at Vic, who had set his drink down and leaned his head back to stare at the ceiling.

Shit! "Okay."

"I met a guy downstairs who said they just had a cancellation and wondered if we'd like to take the appointment for a meeting."

"What kind of meeting?" Lane looked over at Vic.

"Timeshare."

Vic's chin hit his chest. He dropped his gaze, closed one eye, then focused on Lane. "Give it half an hour and she'll have yours in her hand." He grabbed his crotch and pumped it up and down.

Arthur stood up. "They'll see us in five."

Lane shook his head and took a deep breath. "No."

Arthur leaned forward until Lane could feel his breath on his ear. "Alejandro set this up. We'll meet our contact in plain sight."

Lane rolled his eyes for Vic's benefit, drained his cappuccino, grabbed his laptop, stood, then followed Arthur to the elevator. They went up to the first floor and were greeted by a man with a receding hairline, slicked-back grey hair, thick round glasses and a hooked nose. Lane was reminded of one of the pelicans he'd seen on the beach. "Name's Bob.

You must be Lane and Arthur! Come on in guys. I've got a few things to show you, and then we'll have some breakfast at the members' restaurant."

Turn down the volume, Bob! Lane thought before tuning out after about thirty seconds into the spiel. He watched Arthur, who seemed comfortable with the volume and volubility.

They sat down for brunch near the beach under a thatched roof. The wind rolled over the waves, then the beach; it tugged at Lane's shirt. Arthur arrived with a bowl of yogurt and fresh fruit. Bob said, "If you become a member, you get all of the best food."

Lane got up and went to get breakfast at the buffet. He blinked away the beginnings of a headache. There was the usual lineup for tacos so he went for the fresh fruit and vegetables instead. *You know you're getting old when the fresh fruit and vegetables begin to look better than the bacon and fried potatoes.* He returned to the table.

Bob stood. "Excuse me while I get a bite to eat."

Arthur raised his eyebrows and looked at Lane, who shrugged and popped a slice of melon in his mouth. The sprinkle of lime juice on the fruit made for a delightful combination of flavours.

Arthur used his fork to point at the beach. "The whale is gone."

Lane looked as another wave curled, the wind carried a white mane of spray out to sea and the water crashed against the sand. He felt the shudder of the concussion through the soles of his sandals. "I could get used to a place like this."

"I think the kids would like it here. Provided of course someone's not setting fire to the place, murdering a mistress or killing the whales."

Lane nodded, speared a morsel of pineapple and popped it in his mouth.

Bob set his plate down, pulled up his chair, set a napkin in his lap and bowed his head in prayer. He looked sideways to see whether his clients had noticed, then leaned back and asked, "How's the food?"

He checked to make sure we noticed he's a good, trustworthy Christian. "Food's great." *Now my mind is on red alert.*

Bob talked before and after bites, then took them up to the show suite. Next door to it was a two-thousand-square-foot suite being repaired by half a dozen tradesmen. Bob said, "Doing some renovations."

Lane leaned to look into the suite, saw a door kicked off of its hinges and a shattered sliding glass door leading to a deck running the width of the building. "Is that where Fuentes stayed?"

Bob blushed before ducking into an adjacent door and the show suite. "This is the kind of room you'll be staying in."

Lane walked in, tuned Bob out and stepped onto the balcony. He looked out at the waves and the spot where the humpback calf had washed up. Five minutes later, they were sitting at a table in the timeshare sales room. Bob and another salesman named Carlos were across from them. Behind them, in the corner, were two walls of one-way glass. Lane heard Arthur say, "No, thank you." Lane tuned completely out and thought about the events from the last couple of days — until the third sales representative threw his papers and phone on the carpet. Lane studied the man. He weighed maybe one hundred fifty pounds and wore a blue tie, a white shirt, perfectly coiffed hair and poker-player sunglasses. The hair looked like it might have come out of the second shelf of his refrigerator. Lane read *Luis* on the man's nametag.

Arthur stood up.

Luis nodded at the glass walls behind them. "You are embarrassing me in front of my boss." His voice was low and thick with a combination of anger and ersatz pleading.

Lane studied the man's eyes. They were green, and his face was shaved so close it shone.

Arthur said, "We're not buying today. Some disconcerting things happen at your resort."

"Buying a timeshare saved my parents' marriage." Luis leaned in closer, his eyes staring. Lane recognized the look of calculated intent he'd seen many times before in an interrogation room or at church. "My father was always working. My mother made him buy a timeshare and insisted we spend a month together as a family."

"We're not buying today," Arthur repeated.

Luis turned to Arthur. "I've heard that before from people who ended up buying."

Lane shook his head. Arthur sat back in his chair and crossed his arms.

A smiling man of sixty-five or seventy, with a bit more hair than Arthur, wore a white shirt and no tie. He approached the table and stood next to Lane. "Hello. My name is Marco. We just need to do a quality control survey before you go." He shook hands with both of them.

Lane rolled his eyes. Arthur stood up. "Fine."

Marco smiled. They followed him out of the sales room and down the hallway into a larger room with three empty tables and a reception desk in one of the corners. The room was the colour of coconut shells and the light was subdued. Marco opened his right hand and indicated they should sit down. Lane hesitated. Marco said, "Please."

Lane looked at Arthur, who shrugged then sat down. Lane remained standing and looked at the door. "I'd like to get a cappuccino."

Marco waved at the receptionist's assistant. "*Dos cappuccinos, por favor.*" A tall young man in a white shirt stood up and walked from the room. *They're not going to let us leave the room until we buy something.*

Arthur turned to Lane and winked. He sat down.

Marco said, "We like you to come back. The Mexican government likes you to come back. We have a special offer for sixty-one nights." He flipped over a page on a notepad to reveal some of the details. Arthur leaned forward to read.

Five minutes later Arthur had signed a contract and paid for the timeshare with his gold card. Lane was sipping a cappuccino.

Arthur turned to him. Motion caught Lane's eye. A man in a green shirt and black ball cap followed Luis across the room. The man with the ball cap glanced their way. His hair was black, his shoulders were broad and he walked with arrogant self-assurance even in sandals and shorts. Then he and Luis strode through a door to the left of the reception-ist's desk.

"What?" Arthur asked.

Lane leaned close to Arthur. "That was Sean Pike."

Arthur's eyebrows lifted, and lines crossed his forehead. "I thought you said he was dead."

Lane shook his head. "I think we just found Keystone."

At supper, they sat across from each other in a Mexican-style restaurant where the fish was delicate and the margaritas were deadly. After supper they walked back to their room along the lit pathways. The half moon cast soft shadows over the pool. Alejandro was sitting in one of the deck chairs just outside of their room. He waited for them to come closer. Lane saw the sliding glass door to their room was open. "How did you get in?"

Alejandro wore black. He held up a plastic key card. "You're packed."

Lane pushed the sliding patio door open wider and walked into the room. Both his and Arthur's luggage sat near the door. Alejandro closed the door and used a flashlight to illuminate the room. "What's going on?" Arthur asked.

"My Karen heard Luis — one of the timeshare salesmen — talking with a man he called Pike. Pike said he wants you eliminated tonight." Alejandro pointed at the beach. "Some men are watching the front entrance. I have transportation waiting." He leaned his head to the left.

"Point the light over here, please." Lane went to the safe, took out the laptop and cell phone and put them in his carry-on bag, then stuffed their cash, credit cards and passports in his pocket. "Let's go."

"Just like that?" Arthur asked.

Lane nodded. He listened at the door. Footsteps made a gentle echo in the hallway. Lane pointed at the patio and picked up two bags. He followed Arthur and Alejandro out onto the patio. He saw the black silhouette of a handgun in Alejandro's right hand as he took one of the bags from Lane with his left. Arthur shouldered both carry-on bags and led the way to the beach. They stopped on the ocean side of the rock wall and watched their room. In the foreground, a man and woman stepped out onto the sidewalk. An outside light set half a metre off the ground lit their faces. Her sandals slapped against the sidewalk. No other signs of life were visible.

Alejandro, Lane and Arthur turned and walked through the soft sand toward the white effervescence of the waves and the glow of the half moon on the black water. There was a nicker off to the left, followed by the gentle slapping of metal on leather. Lane spotted the silhouette of one horse then counted five. *You've got to be joking.*

A man in a cowboy hat leaned over the saddle of the lead horse. "Alejandro?"

"Si." Alejandro tied one suitcase to the side of the pack-horse, then took a second bag from Lane and tied it on the other side. Arthur hung the carry-on bags on the saddle horn, stuck his foot in a stirrup and bounced up into the saddle. A wave crashed against the beach.

Alejandro put his hand on Lane's shoulder. "Get on."

Lane shook his head. "This is a bad idea."

Alejandro pulled him closer to one of the horses. "You are from Calgary. It has the Stampede. You must know how to ride."

Lane put his hand on the horse's shoulder and inhaled its scent. He put his left foot in the stirrup. *I've only ever learned how to fall off a horse.* After fumbling around, he finally managed to get his toe in the stirrup, then grabbed the saddle horn and tried to pull himself up. The horse moved sideways, and Lane had to hop on his free leg. Alejandro grabbed the horse's bridle with his left hand, held it still and waited for Lane to heave himself into the saddle. Alejandro handed the reins to Lane, then climbed on the remaining horse.

Lane bobbed atop the horse. Arthur said, "Hold on with your knees."

What the hell does that mean? Lane gripped the saddle horn with both hands.

The now familiar growl of Fuentes's cigarette boat ripped the serenity created by the waves and moonlight.

The man in the cowboy hat said, "*Vámonos!*"

Alejandro and Arthur used their heels to get their horses moving. Lane looked left at the brightly illuminated neighbouring resort. *Those lights will make us easy targets.* His horse began to trot along the hard-packed sand at the edge of the ocean as Lane bounced atop the saddle. The cinch began to slip, and he found himself with his right leg over the horse's back, both arms around its neck and his left cheek against the mane. *Hold on!* The noise of the cigarette boat's engine crackled as it throttled back.

Lane's horse stopped. "Stand up," Alejandro said. Lane touched the sand with his left toe, then allowed his right leg to slide off the horse's back. He looked inland, noticing they were protected by the shadow of a two-storey dune. He looked out to sea and spotted the running lights of the idling cigarette boat. To his left, Arthur, Alejandro and the man in the cowboy hat held the bridles of their mounts. Lane could hear them making soothing sounds to the horses. Out on the water, the moon cast its silver. Further to the right, the lights of Palmilla dotted the hill jutting into the ocean. Alejandro worked on adjusting Lane's saddle.

Lane concentrated on his breathing as they waited in deep shadow hoping no light would find and illuminate them. His horse nudged him with its nose. He spotted motion in the silver water illuminated by the moon. A spray of water. The back of a whale. The flash of gunfire from the cigar boat. The sound reached them seconds later. The moonlit triangle on the ocean was still again. There was a roar as the cigarette boat accelerated, then turned and pounded over a swell, though the moonlight and off in the direction of Cabo San Lucas.

Lane waited. The sound of Fuentes's boat receded. He heard one of the horses swish its tail, followed by the sound of creaking leather, signalling one of the riders was climbing into his saddle. Lane took a long, slow breath, grabbed the reins and the saddle, then stuck his left foot in the stirrup. He hopped alongside his mount as it decided it was time to leave with or without him. Lane managed to yank his foot back out of the stirrup, took the reins and walked alongside, trusting the horse to know where they were heading.

chapter 14

Lane sat in the bow. The fishing boat settled into a trough before climbing the rising swell. He felt a tap on his shoulder. Arthur smiled and handed him a cup of coffee. "Thanks." Lane gripped the ceramic cup and took a sip. *The cook really knows how to make good coffee.* He looked out over the Sea of Cortez and the hazy outline of mainland Mexico's coastline on the horizon.

Arthur pointed at the round-faced man in the wheel-house. "He tried to explain something to me, but it was all in Spanish. I think he was saying something about a boat coming to pick us up."

"I need to go back." Lane closed his eyes and felt the breeze on his face.

"Are you nuts?"

Lane opened his eyes. "Fuentes will have contacts on the mainland. We stand out." He lifted his eyebrows as he looked at Arthur. "The last place they'll expect me is back in San José."

"'*Me*'?" Arthur watched Lane with an ominous intensity evidenced by the deepening wrinkles across his forehead.

"You'll go home and I'll go back." Lane felt the certainty of his decision fade before his partner opened his mouth.

Arthur pointed his finger at Lane's chest. "You think I'm going to go home while you go back?"

Lane nodded.

Arthur shook his head. "Where you go, I go. End of discussion. This is not negotiable. We're going back together."

chapter 15

They landed at Los Cabos airport in the rain. The clouds were grey and the overcast was solid. The wait for their checked baggage was unusually long. Lane shifted the strap of his carry-on bag while Arthur stayed next to him, scanning the people around them. A woman with a sleeping child in a stroller stood beside a man holding a nodding toddler to his chest.

A pair of men were led away by a uniformed guard. One man wore a backpack; both wore ball caps. The guard pointed down a side hallway, and a tourist close to Lane and Arthur laughed loudly. "Those two are going to get the rubber glove treatment."

Arthur didn't move. "That isn't funny at all."

Finally a man in blue coveralls began unloading the baggage. A dog sniffed along the rows of bags and suitcases. It stopped and barked. A police officer stopped to wrap a piece of luggage in a large green bag with white tape, then followed the dog as it moved ahead and barked once more.

Arthur pointed as one of their bags came around the conveyer. He hauled it off the belt while Lane spotted and grabbed the other. They walked side by side through the blinding blue lights and white walls of the timeshare gauntlet, through the sliding glass doors and outside into the heat.

They picked their way through the crowd of travellers, suitcases, drivers and hotel reps. Arthur led the way to a waiting gold Ford van. The driver leaned away from the fender. "You need a taxi?"

Lane read the man's nameplate. "Yes, please, Roberto."

Roberto took their bags and piled them inside the rear doors of the van. Lane and Arthur climbed in and sat next to each other. Roberto drove through town past car repair shops, restaurants, homes and businesses. Some of the intersections were under a foot of water and the vehicles slowed to plow their way through. They drove past the La Luna Cortez resort's barricade and up to the front door. They climbed out and were immediately recognized by a busboy named Gerardo. He had a round, smiling face and powerful shoulders. While Arthur paid Roberto, Gerardo took the bags. "Come with me, señor."

Lane waited for Arthur before following Gerardo. He set their bags on a trolley and led them through the lobby and into a room lined with windows along one wall. There were desks along three walls. A bottle of champagne sat chilling near a pillar in the middle of the room. "Thank you." Lane handed Gerardo a five-dollar bill.

The porter shook his head. "*No gracias.* Mr. Gonzalez told me to watch out for you, that I should take you here, close the doors and wait with you." He walked over and closed the French doors. "Please sit." He gestured at the couch. "Would you like something to drink?"

"Cappuccinos?"

Gerardo lifted a phone receiver and spoke in rapid Spanish.

Arthur remained standing. Lane studied approaching foot traffic through the French doors.

Lane spotted a beefy black-haired man in a blue shirt, black pants and shoes. A pair of security guards who were taller, heftier and wearing white shirts with blue shoulder flashes flanked him. When he stood outside the door, Gerardo announced, "Mr. Gonzalez."

Gonzalez opened the doors. One of the security guards remained outside. The other came inside with Gonzalez, who extended his hand. "*Mucho gusto*, Señor Lane, Señor Merali."

When Lane stepped aside for Arthur to shake hands with Gonzalez, he saw the pearl-handled .45 on the security guard's hip. Gonzalez placed an open palm on his chest. "My name is Aldo and this is Mario."

Lane nodded. Arthur inhaled and released the breath slowly.

Gonzalez continued. "We must wait for someone who speaks better English. His name is Emir."

A moment later, a slender young man arrived. "Yes, you asked for me?" Emir wore glasses and sized up Lane as he stepped into the room before glancing at Gonzalez and the armed security guard. Lane could see half moons of sweat under Emir's arms as his eyes checked passersby.

Gonzalez said something in Spanish and Emir turned to Lane and Arthur. "He says he is a friend of Alejandro Ramirez and Alejandro asked us to watch out for you. He lost track of you and thought you might come back. The people you work for are worried and are waiting to hear from you."

Lane said, "I saw the woman Fuentes had killed. I know about the fire. One of Fuentes's associates recognized me." He pointed at the men in the room, then at his chest. "It's very dangerous for all of us if too many people know we came back."

Emir translated, and they waited for Gonzalez to speak. Lane studied the man's face and saw his brown eyes express both anger and grief. "This resort is owned by my family," Gonzalez said.

Emir raised his eyes as Gonzalez reverted to Spanish. Emir waited, then said, "Celia Sanchez was Señor Gonzalez's niece. He fired Ruben at the front desk because Ruben tried to cover up her murder and helped Fuentes get rid of Celia's body. He understands that you were able to identify her body from photos you took?"

Lane nodded.

Emir asked, "Señor Gonzalez asks if it is possible that she is still alive? His sister has hopes because the body was not recovered."

Lane shook his head. "I'm sorry."

Gonzalez nodded, then held his hand to his chest. He tried to speak, could not, then tucked his chin. It took at least a minute and several attempts for him to be able to speak.

Emir looked at Lane and Arthur. "He says that Fuentes is a *pinche narco* and whatever we can do to help you we will do. He says that Fuentes and a man named Luis Bonner, who owns a big house in Palmilla, pay off some of the local police. Palmilla has its own security force and the police don't go there. Mr. Gonzalez also knows that Fuentes is responsible for the fire at La Luna Cortez." Emir pointed in the direction of the elevators for effect.

Lane looked at Arthur. "You are asking us to put our lives in his hands."

Emir listened, then said, "You returned. You can still go home. We live here. We risk not only our lives but the lives of our families."

The door opened, and Alejandro walked into the room. He looked at Lane and Arthur. "What the fuck are you two doing back here?"

Arthur smiled. "*Mucho gusto*, Alejandro."

Even Gonzalez laughed.

✕

Frederick Lee read the text message on his phone as he walked along the hallway on his way out the door. *Priority contract.*

Detective Paul Lane. Details to follow.

He looked at the time on his phone, then walked to the library. No computers were free, so he stood behind the chair of a boy who wore a football jacket and weighed more than two hundred fifty pounds. The shoulder of his black-leather team jacket said Brett. The side of Brett's head was one straight line to his neck. He spotted Frederick's reflection in the monitor and looked over his shoulder. Frederick raised his eyebrows. Brett turned back to his computer, logged off, got up and walked away.

Frederick logged on with the password of another student; he'd paid fifty dollars for the ID. Then he began a search for Detective Paul Lane.

×

Lane and Arthur sat on the second floor of a French restaurant called Napoleon's. It was across the street from a row of art stores and a glass factory. Arthur broke a piece from a chocolate croissant, then sipped his coffee. Lane sipped a mocaccino; Alejandro, an espresso. The shop windows and streetlights lit the cobblestone street below. Tourists walked from shop to shop and police stood at the intersections.

"The airport has become very difficult, so Fuentes and Bonner had to find a new way to transport their product," Alejandro said.

Arthur wiped his fingers on a paper napkin. "How do these art galleries fit in with the plan?"

Alejandro pointed at a gallery across the street. There were silver letters in the window. "Culiacán Gallery sells African art and paintings by Mexican artists. The African pottery and sculptures are made in Culiacán. The Mexican artists are unknowns. Fuentes has the art made in his home-town and sells it here. Bonner pays millions of dollars for the art but none of it ends up in his Palmilla home. It just ends up in another gallery to be resold to the tourists. It is — how you say, money laundering?"

Arthur nodded. "What else are they into?"

Lane watched as a man and a woman walked into the gallery and began to work their way around. "Bonner has a yacht, a custom home in Palmilla and another in La Jolla near San Diego. Correct?"

Alejandro nodded. "That is right."

Arthur sipped his coffee. "This gallery and the art must be only a small part of their business." He turned to Alejandro. "Does the art business provide economic opportunity for the people in Culiacán?"

Alejandro smiled, holding up a millimetre gap between his thumb and forefinger. "Un poco."

"So they are his slaves. Still, we must be missing a piece. A very big piece." Arthur put his cup down.

Lane looked down to the street. Fuentes walked up the centre of the road. He wore a loose-fitting white shirt and was flanked by bodyguards in black business suits. He climbed the stairs to the gallery and walked inside. The bodyguards took up their positions on either side of the stairway before crossing their hands in front of them.

A few minutes later, Sean Pike and Manny Posadowski arrived. Pike wore a short-sleeved orange shirt. Manny wore his usual red muscle shirt showcasing the tattoos running from wrist to wrist.

"Maybe this will give us a hint," Lane said,

Manny, Sean and Fuentes left about thirty-five minutes later. The bodyguards helped Manny down the stairs because he was listing to the right. Sean waited and accepted the help of the next bodyguard. Fuentes waved away any help, stumbled, righted himself and, with exaggerated care, took each step.

"That is interesting," Arthur said. "What are they carrying?"

"Looks like wine bottles." Alejandro looked at his watch. "I don't think wine makes you drunk that fast."

"Only tequila or scotch would do that to a person." Lane watched Fuentes hand a bottle of wine to one of the bodyguards.

Pike and Manny stood with concentrated stillness at the curb. Each held a bottle of wine protectively cradled in the crook of his right arm.

Arthur asked, "What's so special about that wine?"

A flat-black Ford Expedition pulled up in the intersection at the bottom of the hill. Fuentes climbed in the passenger seat. Manny, Pike and the two bodyguards climbed in the back.

Arthur took a bite of croissant and a sip of coffee. "We may have the solution to our money-laundering problem if we can figure out what just happened."

chapter 16

Lane sat under the umbrella on the deck outside their room. They were now in a suite on the top floor of La Luna Cortez. Mr. Gonzalez told them, "You can enjoy the beach and the sun but no one else will know you are there. That way you will have the least possibility of being seen except by those we trust."

Lane wore a shirt, shorts and sandals and sipped a cappuccino. He opened his laptop and checked his email. The first message was from Matt.

Uncle Lane,

Sam is moping around here missing you guys. He looks out the window every time a car goes by. He misses all of his walks.

Dan came over again last night. While he was here, his sister Linda phoned Christine on her cell. They had this long three-way conversation. Then she hung up, and Dan and Christine had another long conversation.

Apparently Lola phoned Linda and told her that Christine moved out, Dan is sad and you and Arthur are to blame. I know it's bullshit! Lola's playing the victim card. Anyway, Linda phoned to say that she was thinking of seeing more of her nephew and maybe moving back to Calgary. She wants to buy a place. Christine, Dan and Indiana will housesit for her until they get a place of their own. They're upstairs right now looking over the real estate listings. Good news, I think.

School's going well. Hard to believe that I'm graduating soon. Maybe you and Arthur will actually get your house back. It will be a little worse for wear, I'm afraid. Indiana has discovered what markers do to walls! Just joking!

You must be up to something important. Marked and unmarked vehicles cruise by here in a steady stream. No worries about kidnapping this time! (I know, that was a bad joke, but it was meant to put you at ease.)

Matt

Next Lane opened a message from Nigel.

Lane,

Anna has been working some magic up here. She tracked payments into an account accessed by Frederick Lee. Sums of fifty thousand dollars were deposited into the account before and after each of the last gang-related shootings in the last year. The only time he wasn't paid was before and after the shootout and rollover last week.

After a meeting with some of the gang suppression unit officers, we've come to the following conclusions.

1) Frederick Lee is probably working for someone who would benefit from a war between the FOBs and FKs.

2) There have been similar shootings/assassinations in Vancouver.

3) As stated before from wiretap information, you may be one of his targets. Don't worry. We've got Matt, Christine, Dan and Indiana covered.

4) There may be a Cayman connection to the payments made to Frederick Lee.

I hope this brings you up to speed. How are things at your end? You've kind of dropped off the radar and Harper is going nuts.

Nigel

Lane looked out at the ocean. A wave rolled in and dumped tonnes of water onto the beach. A couple ran away from the wave as it swept up the shoreline. He began to type.

Nigel and Cam,

Thank you for keeping an eye on our family.

I don't want to reveal our location. This is a wireless connection and security may be a concern.

Thank you for the Lee information. If possible, please send a picture of him.

We've been working on tracking the finances of the local operation. Perhaps we could communicate through our mutual steampunk friend who may be able to offer more secure communications.

There is a walking, talking corpse down here who is the most likely candidate for the role of Keystone.

Lane

He logged off his laptop and plugged it in to keep the battery charged.

Arthur slid the patio door open. He wore a white house-coat and sandals. "What's new?"

How much should I tell you?

Arthur waved as finger at Lane. "I want to hear it all."

"All?" *Do you really want to know?*

"All of it. And while you're at it, get rid of the beard. There are only one or two other men at this resort with beards. It makes you stand out."

Lane turned to his laptop and opened his email. "You probably need to read this one first." He waited while Arthur read, then opened another message and waited again. He looked out at the ocean and the waves rolling in.

Arthur looked up from the computer. "What do you think?"

Lane thought for a moment. "Pike wants me dead and is looking to control a large chunk of the distribution of drugs in western Canada. He's working with the Angels, who will also want a cut. If we do manage to do something to stop Pike, Posadowski, Bonner and Fuentes, then we leave a power vacuum, which will need to be filled. That's one of the biggest problems. We can arrest one of the players, but someone always comes along to take his place. For instance, when Kevin Moreau and Stan Pike were killed, little brother Sean came along to fill the void. Now he sees an opportunity to become more successful than Moreau ever was. And he has detailed knowledge of how the police operate. That makes him a bigger threat to us and a major asset to people like Fuentes, Bonner and the Angels."

"So why not change the target?" Arthur sat down at the table under the umbrella.

"What do you mean?"

"It's a business for these guys. They are motivated by profit. Take away the profit and they're out of business."

"How do we do that?"

Arthur looked down at the pool where children were not allowed. A group of adults doing water aerobics formed a rough circle in the water. Not one of them was under the age of fifty. "I think we should have this talk with Aldo, Karen and Alejandro. They have the perspectives we need to figure out the best possible option."

"So you have an idea?"

Arthur closed the laptop and handed it back. "I do."

×

They met in the suite just after lunch. Aldo Gonzalez was accompanied by his bodyguard. Emir sat next to them. All three wore the standard resort blue shirts and black pants. Alejandro arrived with Karen moments later. *So she is the one in charge of the timeshare boys!* Lane thought. Karen was dressed in a white blouse, black slacks and sandals. Alejandro made a fashion faux pas by wearing jeans and a red T-shirt.

The talk began as soon as everyone had a coffee or water in hand. They gathered around the dining table.

"Fuentes moved into a house just down the hill from Bonner at Palmilla," Gonzalez said.

"A permanent move?" Arthur sat across from Gonzalez and next to Lane.

Karen pushed her long black hair from her shoulder. "When the narcos move in, it's permanent. They start to intimidate the business owners. They drive their big SUVs and collect money from people nearby who are working hard just to make a living. It's already happening here. Fuentes's men want a percentage from the timeshares we sell. Two of our salesmen now work for him."

Gonzalez wriggled his fingers into the air and said something to Emir, who nodded. "They are wrapping their tentacles around us."

Alejandro said, "Then the narcos sit back on their fat asses while everyone else works for them. The people have no choice because they're too afraid of what might happen to their families if they say no. We've already seen how ruthless they are."

The bodyguard said something in Spanish. Karen pointed at him. "This is Victor. He says that Fuentes's men already killed a restaurant owner in San José. They left his body inside and burned the place to the ground. Now the restaurant and shop owners in San José are saying they have no choice but to pay up. It's the same in San Lucas. Victor's family moved here to get away from all that in his home town in Sinaloa."

Lane put his coffee down. "We have some information on the business that Pike, Fuentes, Bonner and Posadowski are in. We were wondering if you could help us with how best to handle the problem. Arthur —" Lane pointed at his partner "— thinks our best strategy is to go after the money. The big problem is what happens after we deal with the four of them. Usually another crime group moves in and takes over the business. We hope that by working together we might be able to work out a more permanent solution to the problem here and back home in Canada. We are very close to a gang war in our city. Pike comes from Calgary. He has taken over as the head of his family's drug distribution business. Now he seems poised to take control of most of western Canada."

Gonzalez waited for Emir's translation, then asked, "How well do you know this Pike?"

Lane said, "He used to be a police officer, but I don't know him well."

Arthur said, "It appears that Pike has hired a killer to eliminate Lane."

Alejandro smiled. "So you are in the same soup as we are?"

Karen shook her head and looked at Lane. "We are in a mess and you call it a problem. How can we talk about solutions if all our lives are at risk?"

Lane thought for a moment. "I saw what happened to Celia Sanchez. I've seen what people like Pike do. I have a talent for hunting down people like Pike and Fuentes. I think that if we understand the primary problem and come up with a solution, we should be able to eliminate this threat and perhaps future ones as well."

"You haven't dealt with someone like Fuentes before," Alejandro said.

Arthur shook his head vehemently. "Lane hunted down and shot a man who was about to murder a child. He hunted down a man who killed more than twenty-five people both in Canada and in Cuba. He helped get rid of a corrupt police chief." He put his hand on Lane's shoulder. "He can help you hunt down Fuentes and the others."

Karen asked, "You said you wanted a more permanent solution for the problem so that more narcos do not come along to take the place of these men?"

Lane nodded. "That's correct. We need your help to find a way to get rid of the narcos and their profit motive. If they can't make money here, then they will have no reason to be in Los Cabos."

Alejandro leaned his elbows on the table. "So we have to make this place bad for business."

Karen frowned. "But the tourists are good for Fuentes and Bonner's business."

"They are after bigger markets," Arthur said. "This area is one piece in the transportation network. Airport security is becoming problematic, so they are looking at the water. Their boats *Wind* and *Fire* are important tools for transporting. Posadowski and Pike play their part at the other end of the network. If we can figure out how the money works, we should be able to figure out a way to take away the profit."

Karen used an elastic band to tie her hair back. "Money is what motivates them. What would make them walk away from that?"

Lane pointed at her. "We have a plan and hope you can help us with it. There may be a way to reverse the money flow."

✕

"If we follow the plan and it works out, then you know what that means?" Lane sat on the deck as the sun came up. The waves had a silver sheen to them. The wind blew white manes as the waves pounded the beach.

"Things almost never go as planned." Arthur sat next to him. He looked at his watch.

"It means I'll probably need to resign from the Calgary Police Service." Lane sipped the coffee in his right hand, then put the cup on the table.

Arthur didn't answer for a full minute. "It's amazing how the sun gets so hot so fast here. It would be cool back home for at least an hour or two after the sun rises over the horizon."

"Did you hear me?"

Arthur nodded. "Would it be a bad thing if you retired?"

chapter 17

Nigel got the call a little after three in the morning. Anna lay asleep beside him. He walked to the bathroom where his work clothes hung behind the door.

After showering quickly, he brushed his teeth and dropped the toothbrush in the sink. It clattered against the bowl. He grabbed it and waited. Anna's breathing hesitated for an instant; then she fell back to a deep sleep.

Fifteen minutes later he was on Crowchild Trail rising up onto the flyover connecting it to Glenmore Trail. The heated seat was uncomfortable so he turned it off. The exhaust of the car in front of him puffed white.

He crossed over the reservoir bridge. The water was still open. *Not for much longer.*

The condo tower was just beyond Heritage Drive. He pulled up and parked out front. The medical examiner's van — an innocuous black minivan with tinted windows — was parked outside waiting to transport the bodies. The Forensic Crime Scene Unit van was parked next to it. Nigel spotted the death inspector's car.

He climbed out of his Honda Ridgeline and closed and locked the doors. He walked up to the glass front door of the condo tower and stepped into the heat.

"Where's your sidekick?" The uniform at the door had hung her winter jacket on the chair behind her.

Nigel remembered her name just in time. "He's on another job. How are you doing, Harris?"

Harris stood over six foot two, weighed in at a muscular two thirty and had a round face with striking hazel eyes.

She shook her head.

"You were first on the scene?"

Harris nodded. Her face told the rest.

"That bad?"

Harris nodded again.

No smartass macho remarks from her. To her credit, Nigel thought.

"Eighth floor," Harris directed.

Nigel took the elevator. The doors opened. His nose caught the smell first, a raw sewage stink. He looked left. Blood pooled beneath bodies. One of the living, a woman in her late forties or early fifties, lifted her chin in greeting. He recognized the blue eyes of the death inspector, a retired nurse named Linda who often attended events like this. She wore a surgical mask. He caught the scent of tobacco smoke on her as she moved closer. "Five deceased."

Nigel watched as Dr. Colin Weaver photographed the scene in the hallway. Dr. Weaver — or Fibre, as Nigel and Lane called him behind his back — was a whisperer as far as the dead were concerned. His face belonged on the big screen. Interactions with the living continued to mystify him, though. He turned, spotted Nigel, then nodded.

He usually ignores me. If he talks, I have to keep my mouth shut or he'll turn off like a light, leaving this investigation and me in the dark. Nigel waited by the elevator and hoped his nose would adjust to the stink. He saw the feet of one of the deceased who had sagged into the corner by a closed condo door. The body wore a pair of cross trainers with grey uppers and a webbed pattern on the soles.

Fibre turned and approached Nigel. "Dr. Weaver."

"We have one body out here in the hallway," Fibre replied. "The other four are in an adjacent unit. It appears the shooters used weapons with a rapid rate of fire. So far we've collected almost thirty shell casings. The four have multiple wounds. The body here —" he nodded at the young man with black hair, open eyes and a hole in his forehead "— has a single wound."

"Any idea how many shooters?" Nigel asked.

"At least two. Some shell casings are nine-millimetre. Others are forty-five calibre."

Nigel nodded. "Any ID on any of the bodies?"

"All four in the room have been tentatively identified. Two are Vancouver residents, one from Winnipeg and one with an apartment registered in his name. I'll get IDs to you as soon as I'm finished with the pictures." Fibre turned and went back to work.

Five minutes later, a man in a white bunny suit, mask and hood handed Nigel a bag with IDs in it. "You wanna take a look in the condo now?"

Nigel followed the bunny suit down the hallway, past the body in the doorway and into the apartment.

Lane,

Hope you are safe wherever you are.

It appears that the war started by Frederick Lee's employer has escalated. Five people were killed early this morning.

There are several anomalies, which lead me to believe this is a different shooter.

1. It appears there were two shooters. Two different weapons were used. Early indications suggest a Steyr SPP and a Glock .45 were on scene. Both are atypical of our original shooter. Neither weapon was left behind after the killings.

2. It appears four of the victims knew the shooters. The four victims in one unit were on their knees and shot execution style. Each had multiple wounds from what may have been a silenced weapon. The witness called after she heard a single gunshot.

3. The Glock .45 was used to kill the fifth victim who was found outside in the hallway. He was likely unknown to the other victims.

4. So far, we've identified Raymond Lyle of Calgary (he appears to be a bystander); Charles Ford of Vancouver; Nicholas Ford of Vancouver (brother of Charles); Wesley Ng of Winnipeg. The Ford brothers and Ng were all known to police.

5. The fifth victim has yet to be identified.

I have a meeting with Harper and the gang suppression unit in fifteen minutes. I'll keep you informed.

Nigel

×

After reading Nigel's email, Lane stared at Arthur for a long time, then looked out the sliding glass doors to the ocean beyond. "I need a cappuccino."

Arthur looked up from the file he was reading. Gonzalez had brought a folder full of documents obtained from a local business associate. "Feeling like a prisoner already?"

"I said I wanted a blended margarita!" The voice drifted up from below. Lane walked onto the balcony, moved to the railing and looked out between the pool and the red roof of the bar. A man reclined on a blue lounger. He wore a red shirt and white shorts. A broad straw hat hid most of his face except for the tip of a white beard. He was pointing at one of the waiters.

"Sorry, señor," the waiter apologized.

The man with the booming voice looked like a turtle on its back as he struggled to get up out of the lounge chair. The waiter offered his hand. The man slapped it away as the wind blew his hat off.

"My hat! Get my hat!" The man had white shoulder-length hair and a full white beard. The waiter chased the hat onto the beach.

He looks just like —

"Santa. What the hell is Santa doing by the pool?" Arthur asked.

"He's looking for a blended margarita." Lane watched the waiter retrieve the straw hat. Santa grabbed it and pulled it back on his head. The waiter walked to the bar and returned with a margarita. Santa took it, sipped, then waved the waiter away.

"So you're getting to know our regulars?" Karen asked.

Lane and Arthur turned. Karen's hair was tied back with a gold clasp. She wore a red blouse, white pants, red pumps and a gold bracelet on her wrist. *She commands any room she enters*, Lane thought.

"Santa's got a bad attitude," Arthur said.

Karen stood between them and looked over the edge. The air around her smelled of tropical flowers and citrus. "Oh yes, Mr. Kringle."

"You're joking," Arthur said.

Karen shook her head. "That's his name. He comes here every fall and spring. He gets very angry if the waiters get his drinks wrong."

On any femininity scale, Karen is at the top. "He's certainly living up to his reputation."

She laughed. It was uninhibited laughter, the laughter of a confident woman. "I came to let you know that Emir was the architect who designed Bonner's ten-million-dollar home. The work for architects in Palmilla went away so he came to work for us. This is something you need to know?"

Another piece of the puzzle? Lane nodded.

Arthur turned away from the Santa show. "Does he still have a copy of the plans for the house?"

Karen leaned her head to one side. "I'll ask." She turned and walked out past the security guard named Ramón, who smiled for the first time as she passed him.

She makes an exit the same way she makes an entrance: with panache.

Arthur pointed at the Pacific. "Are those the same two whales?"

Lane looked out over the water. The glare was intense, and he leaned left to get his sunglasses from the table. One whale surfaced, then spouted a white cloud. The second whale's back appeared as the first submerged. "I don't know. They seem to be a little close in."

"I've been watching, and they may be the same two who lost the calf. They stay until a boat appears. Then their tails go up and they dive. It's as if they're waiting."

"For what?"

Arthur lifted his cap and scratched the top of his head. "Don't know. It just seems odd."

There was a knock at the door. They both turned. Lane stepped into the room, walked to the front door and waited. There was another tentative knock. He heard the card slide in the lock and saw the handle move. The door opened. Emir stood in front of Ramón, who was looking suspiciously at the black bag in Emir's hand. "Karen sent me here. I have the plans for Casa Bonner on my laptop." He opened the zipper.

Ramón leaned over to look inside, then nodded at Lane. "*Bueno.*" He closed the door and stood back.

"I need to plug in." Emir looked around for an outlet.

"Is the table okay?" Lane walked over to the dining table and pulled out the chair closest to the outlet. Then he walked to the patio door and told Arthur, "Emir's here with the floor plans to Casa Bonner."

Arthur turned with a smile. He jerked his thumb over his shoulder. "Santa's on his next margarita already." He walked inside and closed the patio door.

"Here it is." Emir pointed at the laptop screen.

Lane and Arthur stood on either side looking at the

screen. A series of coloured lines showcased a house at the top of the hill in Palmilla.

"How long is that house?" Arthur asked.

Emir drew a line from one end to the other. "Eighty metres."

Lane looked closely and pointed at what appeared to be a round room. "What's that?"

"The wine cellar. There are shelves of bottles on four sides. The table and chairs are for tasting."

Arthur asked, "How do you get from one room to the next?"

Emir pointed at staircases and walkways. "Almost all access is from the outside along a series of pathways."

Lane leaned closer. "Any safe rooms or hidden storage?"

Emir nodded. "There is a room that he wanted closed up afterward. He didn't like the space. And there is this —" he pointed at a room with eight chairs "— a theatre room. All of the electronics are behind this wall. Another space where something could be hidden."

"Do you have any photographs?" Lane asked.

Emir minimized the blueprint diagram and moved to a collection of photos. "What would you like to see?"

Arthur said, "The hidden rooms."

There was the thump of something heavy striking concrete. Ramón pushed away from the door and rushed across the room. He slid the glass door open; it banged against its stops. Lane followed.

"Sonsabitches! I can have another drink! This is all inclusive! I paid for them!"

Ramón looked over the balcony wall. Lane joined him and looked down at the pool. Mr. Kringle pushed away one of the waiters and sat on the rock wall separating the sand from the patio. A white plastic column lay on its side about a metre away from the pool. "I want another margarita! I'm not drunk!"

The head waiter wore a white jacket. He walked over and stood beside Kringle's waiter, whose hands were on his hips.

Kringle pointed at them. "Get me my drink!"

A boy of five or six wore a red bathing suit. He climbed the steps to the patio and stood near the edge of the pool. "Santa's drunk!"

"I'm not!" Santa stood to prove his point, stumbled, listed sideways, then waved his arms to catch his balance. He managed to regain some semblance of control but continued to lean to the right as he walked along the edge of the pool, slipped on a metal grate and fell. His belly smacked the water. Two waves parted the surface and headed for opposite sides of the pool. For an instant his back was dry; then the water swallowed him. His arms managed enough coordinated movement to get him to the surface. He spat water, coughed and reached the edge. Two arms tried to pull his three-hundred-pound frame from the water and succeeded — sort of. He ended up beached with his belly on the concrete deck while his knees and feet remained in the water.

The two waiters each grabbed one of Santa's arms and heaved him further up the deck. He rolled to one side and lay there catching his breath.

One of the forty-something women, who'd apparently spent much of the afternoon dehydrating and rehydrating herself with various alcoholic beverages, sat up. Predictably, she forgot that she'd untied the top of her bikini to prevent a white line in her tan. Her free breasts danced to their own tune as she sang something vaguely resembling every Christmas ditty ever written.

Arthur and Emir approached the balcony. Arthur asked, "What did we miss?"

Ramón said something cutting in Spanish.

Lane smiled. "Just some drunken fresas."

chapter 18

Frederick Lee sipped a macchiato as he walked through the back entrance to the school. Brittany followed him inside. The leather soles of her red boots met a wet patch on the tiles. She slipped and grabbed his bad arm, nearly spilling his coffee. "Shit!" The pain made Frederick close his eyes. He reached into his coat pocket for a Percocet, popped it in his mouth and took a sip of coffee. The nurse had given him ten painkillers last night. He'd had to return when a fever and chills accompanied the pain. She told him he had an infection and managed to dig out another pellet she'd missed the first time. Then she gave him the Percocet and antibiotics.

"Sorry." Brittany released his arm, took a step away and adjusted the purse on her shoulder. "I thought it was getting better."

"It'll be better soon." He took another sip of coffee and surveyed the faces of the students in the hall. A guy with his ball cap turned backwards spotted Frederick and looked away. It was a reaction repeated along each hallway as they made their way down to the main foyer where Brittany's friends gathered. The girls had marked their territory and it was understood no one else occupied the space in front of the trophies displayed behind glass. Frederick stood with his back to the bricks as Brittany and her friends chatted. Brittany said, "He hurt his shoulder. That's why he looks pale."

Paula, who had been Brittany's friend since kindergarten, asked, "Did you hear about the gang shooting?"

Frederick listened as he watched the people nearby and those just arriving.

Paula continued eagerly. "Five guys dead. They're saying it was gangbangers." All three looked at Frederick, who felt the weight of their eyes.

A kid in the crowd pointed at Frederick before looking away and talking with a circle of friends who leaned in close to listen.

Frederick pulled out his smartphone, tapped the CBC app and began to read the news.

×

Nigel stood next to his desk. Lori stood opposite him with her back to the closed door. She wore black leather boots, black yoga pants and a thigh-length purple tunic. "Any news on our travellers?"

"They're keeping a low profile. I'm working on the assumption that no news is good news." Nigel looked beyond Lori as someone walked past the office.

"What do you need?" Lori asked.

"I think we need to track a cell phone and a vehicle. After what happened last night, we have to get ahead of this suspect before more people die."

Lori nodded. "Nebal and Murdoch will be able to take care of the vehicle tracker. You want to be able to monitor the cell traffic?"

Nigel nodded. "Jean is finished with the paperwork. So we're ready to go."

Lori asked, "We're talking about Frederick Lee?"

"That's right."

She took a long breath before she opened the door. "You'd better call Harper and get some reinforcements down here to help you out with Lane away. It's gonna get crazy busy before this is over. Got anyone in mind?"

Nigel made eye contact. "I might."

×

It was late afternoon when Ramón opened the door and Alejandro walked in. He was wearing a ball cap, a white T-shirt, faded blue jeans and cross trainers. He looked at Lane and Arthur, then said, "Something's happening. You coming?"

"Where?" Lane bent to put on socks and shoes.

"West of here on the Sea of Cortez side of the Baja. Near a place called Bahia Los Frailes." Alejandro looked over his shoulder. "Wear a hat and good shoes."

Arthur came out of the bedroom. He was buttoning his shirt. "What's happening?"

"Okay if I explain on the way?" Alejandro pulled his phone from his pants pocket to check the time.

"How far is it?" Lane grabbed a ball cap and sunglasses. He went to the fridge and scooped three bottles of water.

Alejandro waggled his right hand. "Maybe two hours."

He led them down the elevator, through a back door and along a green tunnel to the employee entrance. A Jeep with a ragtop, open sides and weathered white paint was parked near the loading ramp. Alejandro climbed in behind the wheel, Lane squeezed into the back seat and Arthur sat up front in the passenger seat. They headed east past the white-walled cemetery, then north along side roads until joining a two-lane highway headed roughly north along the eastern coastline of the Baja. The Sea of Cortez glittered as it came into view.

Alejandro said, "Bonner's yacht raised anchor and headed this way about two hours ago. His cigarette boat hasn't been seen for a day. It looks like there's a meet on. The coast on this side has some long stretches of deserted beach."

Lane felt the wind tugging at his clothes. The Jeep was a flock of parts moving together, lifting over bumps, flapping down the longer stretches, leaning into curves and reluctantly climbing hills. "Where do you get these vehicles of yours?"

Alejandro smiled and looked over his shoulder. His teeth seemed whiter because his skin had seen recent sun. "In Mexico it is always important to have friends. Want to drive? I am expecting a call, so it might work better."

Lane nodded. "Sure."

Alejandro pulled over onto a dusty side road. Arthur climbed out, moved the seat forward and Lane stepped out of the idling Jeep. Arthur climbed into the back seat and Alejandro hopped in the passenger seat. Lane got in behind the wheel, adjusted the seat, put on his seat belt, depressed the clutch, shifted into first and eased the pedal away from the floor. The fan belt squealed, the clutch plate shuddered and the engine stalled. He depressed the clutch, restarted the engine and tried again. About ten minutes later, he was getting a feel for the eccentricities of this Jeep. It pulled to the right, liked third gear on the hills and seemed happiest at just under two thousand RPM.

Arthur tapped Alejandro on the shoulder. "What will we be looking for?"

Alejandro shrugged. "Maybe the cigarette boat will be unloading cargo, or they will be fishing, or they may be dropping someone off. It's hard to know for sure. But it feels like something important because they are all on the same boat and headed for this part of the Baja where they can easily transfer cargo from one boat to another without being noticed. Bonner's yacht usually sails up the Pacific coast to San Diego."

Lane looked west at the desert where low shrubs and taller cactus pointed multiple fingers at the horizon.

Alejandro said, "Many of the bigger cactuses are hundreds of years old. They hold many litres of water."

A trio of birds circled just off the highway. "Hawks?" Arthur asked.

Alejandro shook his head. "Vultures."

Lane glanced at the dark-coloured birds with long, finger-like feathers at their wingtips. They rode the breeze coming off the ocean. "It looks like nothing should be living out here."

"The desert is deceptive. There are squirrels, foxes, road-runners, coyotes and some mountain lions. The hunters usually come out at night." Alejandro pulled his phone from his pocket, putting it to his ear. He began to speak in Spanish and looked ahead where the highway followed the coastline. He ended the conversation, put his left hand on Lane's shoulder and pointed up ahead with his right. "You will turn right onto a dirt road less than a kilometre ahead. We have company about ten minutes behind us."

Lane looked in the rear-view mirror but saw no approaching traffic. He shifted into a lower gear and began to decelerate. A few seconds later, he saw the white sand of the side road. He shifted down, braked and eased off the pavement. He drove along a twisting white sand road, rounded a fifty-foot cactus and wound east toward the Sea of Cortez. Alejandro said, "I have a source who says that Fuentes has used this beach before. Once you get to the beach, turn right. There is a building we will be able to park behind."

Arthur asked, "If someone is following us, won't they be able to see our tracks?"

Alejandro shook his head. "Don't worry. After the dust settles behind us and the wind does its work, they won't notice."

Lane turned right. The road opened up onto an undeveloped beach. He shifted into four-wheel drive as the road disappeared and the sand became softer. Atop a hill was a white concrete building with a domed roof. It sat beside a corral made of orphaned planks of grey wood. Lane pulled up on the far side of the building and parked on a concrete pad under a thatched roof supported by six posts.

He shut off the engine and listened to the engine tick as it cooled. Waves pounded the beach. The low sun enriched the colours.

Alejandro climbed out his side of the Jeep and moved the seat forward. Arthur backed out and reached for a bottle of water.

Lane pointed at the ocean. Bonner's yacht *Fire* pushed a hefty bow wave as it motored north. They watched it slow and settle in the water. Alejandro reached into the back of the Jeep, unzipped a backpack and pulled out binoculars. He took a minute to study the boat, handed the binoculars to Arthur who looked and said, "They're getting the helicopter ready." He handed the binoculars to Lane.

Lane adjusted the focus and watched as two men removed the cover from the helicopter. Then he looked at the bridge where he could see the back of a man's head looking east. Lane looked out beyond the stern of *Fire*. No boat was visible, but he did see the white spray from a whale spout followed by a second. "Looks like they're waiting for someone arriving from the east."

"Did you notice the whales?" Alejandro asked.

Arthur tapped Lane's shoulder. "Let me see." Lane passed the binoculars and Arthur asked, "I wonder if it's the same pair from in front of La Luna Cortez."

"Maybe." Alejandro pointed back along the beach, then ducked in behind the building, dragging Arthur by the shirt sleeve. "It's Fuentes's Excursion." The flat-black SUV swayed and bucked, kicked up road dust then slowed in the softer sand along the beach and stopped. The doors opened. Four men climbed out. The pair in the front wore black sports jackets. They took them off and tossed them on the seats.

Arthur watched through the binoculars from behind the corner of the building. "They are armed."

"Recognize anyone?" Lane asked.

"Pike and Manny." Arthur watched as the four men walked to the edge of the ocean.

"The cigarette boat is here." Alejandro lifted his chin. The bow of *Wind* appeared beyond the bow of the yacht. The high-speed craft idled its way to shore.

Arthur said, "Two men are carrying black sports bags."

"Another deal about to happen." Alejandro reached back behind the Jeep's front seat and pulled out a camera with a long lens. He flipped a switch and adjusted the zoom; the shutter began to click.

Lane watched as the cigarette boat idled just beyond the breaking waves. The bodyguards waded out, holding their guns over their heads. They handed their weapons to a man at the stern, then held the bow and stern while Manny and Pike waded out. The pair reached the stern and climbed aboard followed by the bodyguards.

The cigarette boat's engine rumbled as the boat reversed, turned and aimed into a swell, cresting the wave and dropping into a trough. Bonner guided the boat toward the yacht anchored about five hundred metres from shore.

"What do we do?" Arthur asked. "They only have about a hundred metres to go."

The first whale launched itself out of the water between the yacht and the cigarette boat. Forty tonnes of grey–blue was more than halfway out of the water. It rolled and crashed back into the sea within two metres of the cigarette boat. The resultant wave swamped the cabin of the craft. Its bow lifted into the air. The stern sank. The first whale disappeared with a slap of its tail. A second whale surfaced, spouted and began to slap its pectoral fin overtop the men as they splashed in the water. The tail flukes of the first whale surfaced and worked the other side of the boat. The bow of the boat slipped under a swell.

Alejandro asked, "Do you see what I'm seeing?"

"Incredible," Arthur said.

Lane watched as the splashing stopped. Debris floated on the surface and bodies swayed to the motion of wind and waves.

Minutes later, a zodiac appeared from the far side of the yacht. It began a zigzag search of the water between the yacht and the beach.

Minutes after that, the helicopter was in the air and guiding the zodiac. The boat stopped, and a body was pulled aboard. The zodiac headed toward the shore, then stopped again. Another body was plucked from the water. The zodiac zipped back to the yacht while the helicopter continued to search. It settled onto the deck of the yacht as the light began to fade. The yacht's lights came on, illuminating its bridge, bow and stern. It pulled up anchor and began motoring south.

"What's the plan?" Arthur asked.

"We wait until they are out of sight," Alejandro replied.

"Then what?"

Alejandro watched the yacht through the long lens of his camera. "We see if the keys are still in the Excursion."

They waited until the yacht disappeared around the point. Lane started the Jeep and drove to the black Excursion. In the fading light, Lane turned on the headlights, illuminating the Ford's driver-side door. Alejandro climbed out and tried all four doors. He shook his head. Arthur climbed out and walked to the beach.

Lane pulled on the emergency brake and left the Jeep's engine running. He followed Arthur to the water where two bodies lay rocking in the waves pounding the beach. One man wore a white shirt and an empty holster. His head lay at a right angle to his body. The other body was much bigger. Lane thought he caught the red of a tattoo on one bicep. Arthur went to the smaller body. "Help me." He grabbed one arm and began to drag the corpse up onto the sand.

Lane grabbed the man's other arm. It was broken. "Be careful or you'll pull the arm off." He gripped the collar of the man's shirt instead. "What are you doing?"

Arthur reached into the man's pant pocket. "The keys." He lifted his right hand. Lane heard a jingling sound. Arthur aimed his right hand at the Ford. There was a click. The Excursion's yellow parking lights flashed.

Alejandro moved to the driver's door and opened it. "Let's go!" He pointed at Lane. "Okay if you drive the Jeep back?"

"Yep." Lane began to walk up the beach and away from the water. He headed for the Jeep while Arthur walked toward the Excursion.

When Arthur got there, Alejandro held up a black sports jacket and pointed at him. "Try this on?"

Arthur asked, "Why?"

Alejandro's white teeth shone in the night. "Because you look more Mexican than your fresa boyfriend."

Arthur took the proffered jacket and tried it on. The sleeves were short. Alejandro said, "Just keep your hands down."

Lane pulled up next to the Ford. Alejandro turned to him. "Follow us to Palmilla?"

"Okay." Lane waited for Alejandro to drive away before following about a hundred metres behind so the road-dust had a chance to settle. He was reaching for a bottle of water by the time they found the pavement. He tried driving, shifting gears, twisting the top off the water bottle, then put the bottle in the cup holder until he had worked the Jeep up to over one hundred kilometres an hour. He had it aimed more or less between the centre line and the edge of the pavement. He tried to loosen the cap on the water bottle with his right hand, eventually succeeded, tipped back the bottle and spat water and road dust onto the highway. Then he worked to get the Jeep back in the middle of the lane and about two hundred metres behind the tail lights of the Excursion. They remained that way in the deepening darkness until they reached the outskirts of San José. After that it was stop and go with traffic and streetlights. They were able to move faster as they travelled west on the four-lane highway to Cabo San Lucas. Its surface made the Jeep dance and Lane's teeth rattle. They took the Palmilla overpass and entered a tunnel formed by palm trees along either side of the road. The Excursion turned left down to the beach. Lane followed, pulling up alongside. Alejandro opened the driver's window. "Just park it over there by the surf shop and get in the back." He jerked his thumb over his right shoulder.

A minute later, Lane climbed in the back seat where cool leather and plenty of legroom added to the luxurious feel of a climate-controlled environment. "How will we get through security?" he asked.

Alejandro reversed, turned and headed back away from the beach. The headlights cut a swath through the darkness. "The windows are tinted and I'm betting he'll let us through just because he doesn't want to piss off Fuentes."

They approached the security hut. The lights illuminated a tall man in a white shirt and black pants. He looked at the vehicle then turned to lift the barrier. Alejandro raised his left hand with a wave that blocked his face as he drove through. The Excursion's V8 roared as the SUV climbed the steep grade past closed gates on either side of the road. When they reached the top of the hill and the gates of Casa Bonner, Alejandro used the remote on the visor to open the gate, eased into the courtyard and parked between twin palm trees and in front of the main doorway framed with pink cantera stone. They climbed down from the SUV and walked to the main passageway. A floral design made of many small stones was set in the middle of the pathway leading to the pools with blue light shining up from their bottoms. Below, the ocean lay black and deep; beyond that, the winking lights of the resorts of San José.

Arthur waited as Alejandro used a key to open one of the French doors on either side of the entrance. Then he said, "I think we should try the theatre room first." They looked inside the living room, then up at the pyramid-style ceiling. The furniture was handmade.

They took the walkway along the side of the building. Arthur counted doorways. "I think this is it." He tried the door. It opened into a room of eight reclining leather chairs with metre-wide seat cushions. A curved two-metre screen was mounted on the wall. "There's a space for all the electronic equipment behind that one." He walked over to the TV and began to inspect the wooden panel to the right. Alejandro looked at the panel on the left. Arthur's panel opened; he crouched and eased his right side in until he sat on the sill. "There's a light switch in here." He inched forward.

"Anything there?" Lane asked.

Arthur said, "Not so far."

Alejandro's phone rang. Lane shivered with tension and looked at his friend as he answered in rapid-fire Spanish.

Lane waited until Alejandro had pressed end on his phone. "Any idea how much time we've got?"

Alejandro raised the phone in his hand. "The yacht will probably dock in thirty minutes near San Lucas. They have requested an ambulance. I would guess that we have at least an hour. It will take them twenty minutes to get here by car."

Lane said, "I'm going to take a look around. You and Arthur have lots to keep you busy in here."

Alejandro nodded, handing him the keys. "Just be careful. We may be visible from below and from a distance with all of the lights in this place."

Lane nodded, stepped outside and closed the door. Stairs on his right led to the second floor. To his left a flat sidewalk wound in and around palm trees, bougainvillea and fountains. Spotlights recessed in the tiled walk lit flowering plants. He walked toward the centre of the house and looked inside the office, which was separate from the rest of the building. He walked beyond the office as he tried to remember Emir's floor plan and opened another French door set in a stone wall. Inside was a round table with six leather chairs. He could see bottles of wine stacked on wooden racks crisscrossing the facing wall. The room smelled of polished wood and leather with faint undertones of fermentation.

Lane walked over to the nearest rack, slid a bottle of wine out and checked the label. It was a 1973 Chablis. He slid the bottle back and stepped away, looking for anomalies. *Why did Manny and Pike leave Bonner's art gallery with wine bottles?*

He turned to the next rack looking for unusual corks or colours among the different vintages and brands. *Bonner is a numbers guy.* He counted five from the top and five across, tapped the top of one bottle and slid it out. He went through the entire fifth row without finding anything unusual. It was on the seventh row that he found the Cayman Chablis. Two rows directly below that he found a Geneva Sauvignon Blanc. He set the pair of bottles on the table and sat down. He leaned one bottle over so he could see the label. *How many numbers in a normal UPC code?* He texted his location to Alejandro.

Moments later the door opened. Arthur stepped inside followed by Alejandro. "What have you found?"

Lane held up the Geneva. "This one says it's from the Credit Suisse Winery in Geneva Switzerland." Then he pointed at the Chablis. "It's from the Butterfield Winery on the Cayman Islands."

Arthur reached out with his right hand. "Let me see that." He looked at the label, then studied the bottom of the bottle. He examined the label again. "Can I see the other one?"

Lane handed him the Sauvignon Blanc. Arthur repeated his examination.

Alejandro asked, "What do you see? Are there diamonds inside of the wine?"

Arthur shook his head. "No. It looks like the winery indicates a bank and the bar code — or at least what appears to be a bar code at first glance — is actually an account number." He pointed at Lane and Alejandro. "Could you check whether there are any more Geneva or Cayman labels?"

It took nearly forty minutes to check each bottle, but they ended up with twenty-two bottles of wine, which identified four banks and twenty-two separate account numbers.

Arthur turned to Lane. "Can you call Anna? I need her to check some numbers."

Lane pulled out his phone, checking the face. "We're almost out of time."

Arthur nodded.

Lane dialed zero zero one and then Anna's number. It rang seven times.

"Lane?" Nigel answered.

"Yes. I'm sorry it's late but we can't wait. Is Anna awake?"

There was a pause before Nigel asked, "Where are you?"

"Palmilla. Is Anna available?"

"Palmilla?"

Lane waited. He heard a growling noise. "Not now, fuck face!" There were more muffled sounds before a raspy female voice said, "Lane, if it was anyone else I would tell you to kiss my —" A lengthy pause. "What is it?"

"Do you have a computer handy?"

"Always."

"Arthur needs you to take a look at something." He handed the phone to his partner, who explained the label of one bottle to Anna. He waited while she worked. He looked at Lane. "This is going to cost us a very fancy dinner."

Lane nodded.

Arthur listened as Anna spoke. He pressed END and handed the phone back to Lane. "She says that she needs a couple of hours to get set up and enter the account. In the meantime she wants us to get to another computer to access some data. She also needs the information on the other accounts so she can transfer funds."

Lane turned to Alejandro. "Can you phone Aldo Gonzalez and ask him to get the computers set up? We've got work to do."

Alejandro pulled out his phone. "We need to move. Can you find something to put the wine bottles in?"

They wrapped the bottles in towels they found in the bathrooms, and set them in the back of the Excursion.

Alejandro's phone rang as they were climbing into the SUV. He listened more than he talked. When he spoke, he turned the key in the ignition. He finished with "*Gracias.*" He handed his phone to Arthur and reversed. "Fuentes is dead. Pike has a dislocated shoulder. They are on their way back from the hospital." He moved forward, reversed again, then pointed the nose of the SUV at the front gate. He reached up and used the control on the visor. The gates swung open. "We'll go to the beach and transfer the bottles to the Jeep. We'll leave this beast there."

Arthur asked, "Then where do we go?"

Alejandro wiped tears from his eyes. "Aldo is setting the computers up in your room. They are waiting for us to get to work."

Lane leaned forward and put his hand on Alejandro's shoulder. "You okay?"

"The *pendejo* is dead. I have waited for this day since he killed my mother and sister. At times I thought it would never come. I'm having flashbacks about what Fuentes did to my family." He shrugged Lane's shoulder away. "There is much work to do."

Lane asked, "Any word on Bonner?"

Alejandro said, "Just Fuentes and Pike. We saw Manny's body at the beach. They may not have recovered Bonner's body yet." He looked at Arthur. "Put that jacket on. The windshield isn't as dark as the side windows." He drove through the open gate, then shifted into low gear so that he could drive slowly down the steep grade and around the switchback turns. At the bottom, he stopped at the security gate where the guard nodded and lifted the barrier. Alejandro waved, turned left and then right, bumping down the dirt road to the beach where he parked beside the Jeep.

A little over thirty minutes later, Alejandro pulled up next to the loading dock at La Luna Cortez resort. Lane checked his phone. *No time for sleep tonight.*

The pair pulled up in a late-model Land Rover. One was clean-shaven and wore a button-down shirt and blue slacks. The other wore a long-sleeved black T-shirt and jeans; his long salt-and-pepper hair was pulled back into a ponytail. They climbed out of the Land Rover, shut the doors, set the alarm and walked to the front door of Franco's. The restaurant served some of the best seafood, pasta and pizza in Calgary. They strolled through the front door and upstairs past the sign requesting they wait to be seated. They found a table for four in the corner next to the kitchen and waved the waiter over. Button-Down said, "We need two lagers, menus and Nando the manager."

The waiter nodded. He returned with menus and two beers; a minute later Nando arrived. He had thick black hair and a spare tire pushing against his white shirt and over the belt around his grey slacks. He stood between the men. "I'm here."

Button-Down sipped from his beer then set it down slowly. "We made you a business proposition last week. It's a fair offer for security and piece of mind."

Nando nodded. "The owner asked me to call him when you returned." He pulled a cell phone from his pants pocket. He pressed a button then put the phone to his ear. "They're here." He listened, pressed a button on the phone and palmed it. "He'll be here in fifteen minutes. Could I buy you both the seafood linguini? It's especially good this evening."

Button-Down nodded. "And refill our beers," Ponytail said.

Nando nodded at the waiter before turning and walking through the swinging doors and into the kitchen.

The men waited for their refills.

"What do you think, Robbie?" Ponytail asked.

Robbie looked at his beer. "When we finish this deal, we'll be close to our quota."

"There's something else. A quick job."

Robbie leaned closer and dropped his volume. "What, Daryl?"

"Pike upped the contract on Lane. First one to get a confirmed hit on the target gets a bonus."

"How much?"

"Hundred thousand and two weeks in Cancun."

Robbie sat back. "Do we have a shot at it?"

"If Lane makes it back here from Cabos. There are already a couple of full-patch members down there on the job."

Robbie raised his beer. "Here's hoping the target makes it home."

Daryl lifted his beer and smiled. "*Dos cervezas*."

×

Alex Rendon stretched his legs out and picked up the phone. He watched the quartet of computer monitors in the spare bedroom of his penthouse suite atop a downtown condo.

Nigel answered his phone. "Rendon?"

Alex stood up. At six foot five, his head came close to touching the light hanging from the ceiling. "I'm sending you one minute of sound and video."

"Where was it taken?"

"You know Franco's in Kensington?"

"Yep."

Alex took off his glasses and rubbed the bridge of his nose. "I set up camera and sound because the Angels are trying to shake down the owner for protection money. They also discussed a hit on Lane."

"Who's behind the contract?"

"Pike."

Nigel took a breath. "Send the evidence to me and to Harper. Thanks for this."

"No worries." Alex ended the conversation.

chapter 19

The sun was midway in the sky as Lane leaned on the balcony railing. Below, Mr. Kringle was propped on his blue chaise longue with four empty plastic glasses on a side table. He sipped from a fifth. The pool was empty. Waiters went from fresa to fresa serving drinks and collecting empties. Lane looked out over the ocean to check whether any whales were on the horizon. A savoury blend of seafood, rice and cilantro brought his attention back to the patio where a pan the size of a dinner table sat atop a grill. People lined up for paella. Kringle was on the scent. His generous belly, white mane and red shirt joined the line for food.

Arthur came to stand beside Lane. There were dark smudges under his eyes. He took the cappuccino from Lane's hand and had a sip. Lane asked, "Is it done?"

Arthur handed back the cup, closed his eyes and leaned back to stretch his arms. "The cooperative in Culiacán will support the workers who make the art for Bonner and Fuentes's shops. It will also fund the construction of two schools. Five schools in San José have similar deals arranged with budgets to sustain them, along with breakfast and lunch programs. All of the money from the various accounts has been transferred out. The way it's structured, the money will stay to support the communities and sustain their economies. It's been a good day."

Lane nodded. "Is Anna offline?"

"Just now. I don't know how she did it, but she was able to transfer the money out of Bonner's various accounts and put it in the ones created in Mexico. And she declined to take a percentage."

Lane closed his eyes, leaning his head back to take the full effect of the sun on his face. "It's remarkable that she is one of the most honest people I've ever met even though what she does is illegal."

"You're worried about what we've done?"

Lane shook his head. "Not at all. In fact, I feel something like relief. And I feel good, like we've been part of something that will make a difference."

"Alejandro says there will be lots of questions because the money is gone."

Lane looked at Arthur's rumpled white shirt and khaki shorts. "How much was there exactly?"

"A little over three point five billion in US funds."

Lane smiled. "There will be hell to pay when we get home. The Mexican government will talk to the Canadian government, and they will talk to Alberta's solicitor general. The RCMP will probably get involved."

"You're enjoying this?"

"Why not? The money is going to the people who need it most. Three of the four guys organizing a drug cartel are out of action. A pretty good outcome."

"You think they'll come after you?"

"I *know* they'll come after me. It's time to call Harper, and then Tommy Pham, and let them know what's happened."

×

Lane and Arthur walked along the open corridor, past the check-in desk and through the sliding glass doors. The lights were on in the courtyard and traffic rattled beyond the guardhouse and the one-armed barrier.

"Where do you want to go?" Arthur asked.

"Why not walk up to San José?" Lane spotted Mr. Kringle as he opened the door of a Ford van. It sagged to the curb, bouncing back when the white-bearded man stepped out and shut the door. The gold taxi began to pull away. It braked and its nose dove.

There was the rumble of a pair of pounding motorcycle pipes. Lane, Arthur, the guard at the gate and every other person on the street watched as a pair of Harleys blasted up alongside the taxi and stopped just in front. The biker on the far side looked ahead. The biker on the inside reached into a black bag slung on the side of the gas tank. The shine of silver glowed in the streetlight as a muzzle flashed twice. The Harleys' engines muffled the sharp explosions.

Lane shoved Arthur behind the guardhouse. The Harleys' engines roared and rubber screamed. Lane poked his head around the corner. Mr. Kringle lay on his side. Smoke from motorcycle rubber obscured the scene. The bikes headed west toward the cemetery.

The taxi driver, a couple on their way back from the bar across the street and the security guard made it to Kringle's side before Lane, who spotted two holes in the man's red shirt. The ambulance arrived ten minutes later — three minutes too late.

×

Alejandro knocked on the door and was allowed in by a pair of bodyguards. "You two packed?"

Lane was on the balcony listening to the waves roll in. Arthur was inside checking the safe to make sure they had their passports. He turned to Alejandro. "What's up?"

Alejandro lifted his chin at Lane on the balcony. "Is he okay?"

"I think so. Aldo told us that he thought the killers were looking for a guy in a beard, so he's a bit conflicted. Lane's happy to be alive yet feeling he's somehow responsible for Kringle's death."

"Kringle was a *pendejo*, if that helps. He's been bullying the staff for years." Alejandro walked to the patio door. "Lane? Aldo has arranged for you two to fly to San Diego. He has an old friend who is flying back in a company plane." He looked at the clock by the bed. "We need to hurry."

The men walked down the hallway sandwiched between the bodyguards. They hustled down four flights of stairs, through a set of doors, along a green corridor and out onto the loading dock where they waited outside. Lane looked up and down the lit driveway. He listened for the approach of any vehicles.

Alejandro's phone chirped. He looked at the screen. "Looks like they just arrested the killers. They were headed north on the highway on the way to La Paz."

Arthur asked, "So that's that, then?"

"Not exactly." Lane read a message on his own phone. He showed it to Arthur, who handed it to Alejandro.

A silver four-door BMW X5 pulled into the driveway. One of the bodyguards said something in Spanish.

Alejandro put his hand on Lane's shoulder. "This is your ride, my friend."

The bodyguards lifted the bags into the back. Lane and Arthur climbed inside; Alejandro sat next to the driver, whose seat was moved close to the wheel and raised to its maximum height; even so, the driver's head just cleared the top of the wheel. "*Mucho gusto, señores.* I am Aldo's brother-in-law, Fidel." He backed up, eased up the hill to the gate, checked for traffic and drove north into San José.

Alejandro kept his eyes moving from the traffic ahead to the side-view mirror. "A customs officer will be waiting at the plane. It's at the north end of the airport."

Arthur turned to Lane. "You're not saying much."

"I'm trying to plan ahead. Who will be waiting for us at the San Diego airport? How will we get to Calgary after

San Diego? The Mexican government will probably say the money belongs to them. Bonner's assets in La Jolla will probably be seized by the FBI. If and when we get finished with the FBI, the RCMP will probably investigate. I'm just trying to figure a way through it all."

Arthur nodded. "I thought that's why we need Tommy Pham. He's the lawyer."

Lane's pulled the phone out of the side pocket of his carry-on bag and tapped the screen. He reread the text from Nigel: *Pike has expanded the contract on you and increased the reward. Provide updates on your status so protection can be arranged.*

Arthur leaned over and read the text. "What do you want to do?"

Lane shrugged. "Nigel and Cam will take care of it."

Fidel approached the south end of the airport as Alejandro's phone rang. After a brief conversation in Spanish, he turned in his seat. "The Policía Federal are at the hotel asking for you." He turned to Fidel. "We must hurry."

Ten minutes later they pulled through a gate at the north end of the airport. Fidel stopped at the edge of the pavement and next to a white Bombardier jet with its engines tucked near the tail. Lane got out and went to the back of the SUV. Fidel remotely opened the hatch. Lane shouldered his carry-on, then lifted both of the larger pieces from the back. Arthur and Alejandro joined him.

"Let me help you," Alejandro said. "There isn't much time. You may have as many as three governments after you as we speak."

Lane lifted the handle on his rolling luggage. "Those problems can be managed."

Arthur followed behind. "Then there is no need to rush."

Lane stopped and turned, looking at Alejandro and Arthur. "Pike will be on his way up the coast on Bonner's yacht. He is the priority problem we need to solve." He stood at the open side door of the jet. The co-pilot stepped down and took the first bag. Lane thought, *Until Pike is dealt with, my family will be at risk. I'll take him out first; maybe then it will be time to retire.* "Come on, Arthur. You and I have some planning to do."

chapter 20

Lane finally had the feel of the motorhome. It was thirty-eight feet long, painted gold and called *American Revolution*.

"Are we out of Utah yet? Are we legal here?" Arthur sat on the couch behind the driver. He sipped from a bottle of water.

"Just. Another hour and we should be in Pocatello, Idaho."

"Okay if we stop for something to eat?" Arthur came forward and dropped into the passenger's chair. "What did Nigel call this?"

"Dumbspicuous consumption."

"I don't think I've ever sat in a more comfortable vehicle."

"No way we're gonna buy one of these."

"I'm just saying." Arthur looked out the massive windshield. "How much trouble are we in?"

Lane reached down to fiddle with the power settings on the seat. A pair of full-size silver Chevy SUVs passed them. *Brigham Young University Volleyball* and *Girl Power* were written in pink on signs on the rear windows. "Three governments, the Angels and Pike are after us. I'm starting to think that maybe it's a good thing."

"How do you come to that conclusion?"

"Ever since I signed up with the police service we've been fighting this war on drugs. This time we got together with people from the affected communities and figured out a different solution. Instead of the money going to some federal government, it goes to local communities. The whales took care of some of the heads of the organization. So this may be an opportunity."

"I forgot to tell you that Nigel and Lori sent texts." Arthur held up Lane's phone.

"And?" Lane looked ahead to the semi with two trailers beginning to slow as it climbed a hill. He checked his mirror and moved over into the passing lane.

"They're getting inquiries from the RCMP and FBI. They want to know what happened to Bonner's accounts and they want to talk with you and me."

"Sometimes doing the right thing stirs up a real wasp's nest of trouble. The people who've been fighting the drug war with the same tired old tactics are upset."

"Then there are all of those other people who helped us out. Aldo's friend with the jet who set us up with this delivery to Calgary. The people at the resort. It's like there's this network of people willing and ready to change things — and taking risks to help us change things."

"Kind of like Uncle Tran?"

"Exactly. People with money or connections who are looking for solutions. They're not interested in doing things the same old way. They just see the job that needs doing and then figure out ways to get it done."

Lane nodded. "That's what I've been thinking about. After a while, swimming upstream just gets old."

"What are you thinking?"

"We've tried something new with the supply side. Now we need to take care of the distribution side. Pike's network needs to be dismantled. The problem is what do we replace it with? In San José there was a plan to put the money into the community. What do we do at our end?"

Lane waited until they passed the semi on their way up the hill. "We got rid of Moreau and Stan Pike. Now we have the start of a gang war because Sean Pike wants to expand his market share. With Bonner, Fuentes and Manny out of the way, Pike could end up running the whole mess.

Judging by the way he's operated things so far, it will probably become more violent."

Arthur looked west at the setting sun. "After we stop, you want me to drive for a while?"

Lane checked his mirrors, signalled and eased back into the right lane. "Sure. I might take a nap. You'll wake me when you get tired?"

"I just woke up, so I should be good for a while."

chapter 21

Lane woke up when Arthur stopped in Butte, Montana. The gas station lights were on and the eastern sky was a horizon-wide valance of purple and pink. He put his feet on the floor.

The door of the RV opened, and Arthur climbed aboard. "You're up. Want to get some breakfast?" He sat sideways in the driver's seat. "There's a nice little place between here and the highway." The diesel clattered to life. Arthur checked for traffic before rolling them out onto the road.

Up ahead a neon sign announced that Red's was open. It was a one-storey, flat-roofed, plain white building set at one corner of a parking lot. Arthur manoeuvred the RV alongside a semi parked next to a chain-link fence at the furthest end of the lot. He waited for Lane to open the door, then followed him outside. The air added frost to their breath and they dodged patches of ice as they walked to the front door of the restaurant. The inside was bright, and the decor featured clear-stained shades of softwood, pillars of cedar to support the roof and pictures of highways during every season and from a variety of climates. A shining vintage Harley was parked out front of the kitchen. The waitress wore jeans, a white T-shirt and big blonde hair. She smiled and opened her right hand to indicate they should pick a table on their left. They sat down near a window. The waitress arrived with menus and a carafe of coffee. "When you decide just give me a wave." She left behind the carafe and a pleasant scent of soap and gentle perfume.

Lane poured, added sugar and cream to his coffee, stirred, sipped and smiled. "This is good." He looked at Arthur, who was checking out the room.

"Someone is a pretty good photographer." He pointed at a shot of Moraine Lake. The glacier fed impossibly blue water.

Lane looked at the menu and made his choice. "How come you didn't wake me up to spell you?"

"You needed to sleep and I needed to think."

"About what?" Lane reached for the carafe and refilled both cups.

Arthur reached for a creamer. "The kids are all going to be out on their own. You're about to retire and I was thinking about what we could do next." He looked over his shoulder for the waitress, who headed their way. "You ready to order?"

"What's good?" Arthur asked.

She smiled. "Everything."

Lane ordered bacon and eggs over medium; Arthur, the Montana omelette.

They sipped their coffees in comfortable silence. Lane began to wake up and Arthur surveyed the counter and the kitchen.

The waitress smiled as she set their plates in front of them. Lane sprinkled salt and pepper on his eggs. Arthur watched as the waitress went to the cash register, picked up a tablet and began to tap the screen. She studied something on the tablet, held it up and looked at Arthur. She looked away quickly, then elbowed her way through the double swinging doors into the kitchen. Arthur waited until the cook's face appeared. He was framed in the opening in the wall between the kitchen and dining area. The man spotted Arthur and ducked back behind the wall.

Arthur concentrated on pouring fresh coffee into his cup and Lane's. "Keep eating." Lane looked up. Arthur said,

"Just keep eating." He picked up his knife and fork, cut off an omelette tail and shovelled it into his mouth.

Lane's eyes looked to the left. He looked back at Arthur and raised his eyebrows.

Arthur chewed, took a sip of coffee and rubbed his hand over his upper lip. "The cook and the waitress have taken a sudden interest in you and me. Think it's time to contact Harper and let him know where we are?"

Lane put a slice of bacon on a piece of toast and folded it in half. "Looks like it."

Lane drove the morning. Arthur slept until early afternoon. They stopped for gas and coffee in Lethbridge. Arthur took over in the driver's seat, sipping a cappuccino set in a handy cup holder. He looked at the stubble in the fields sticking out of the snow like fingers. "I know a shortcut." Arthur signalled and turned north onto Highway 23. The two-lane blacktop was a bit of a squeeze for the motorhome. "This will save us at least twenty minutes."

Lane sat beside in the passenger seat, nursing his mocaccino. His stomach growled. "Anything in the fridge?"

"Some apples, I think."

Lane got up and swayed back to the fridge. Inside he found half a dozen apples. "Want one?"

"Later." Arthur lifted his coffee while keeping his eyes on the road. They passed farms and a few pickups headed in the opposite direction.

Thirty minutes later Arthur said, "Keep your eyes open for Highway 529 West."

They spotted the sign at the same time. Arthur slowed, braked then turned west on another two-lane highway.

Robbie sat in the driver's seat with Daryl perched on the passenger seat. The black Suburban's oversized eight-cylinder engine was running. The seats kept their backs and backsides warm, but the leather complained when they moved. They were parked on the north side of a block-long metal-walled building with a corrugated metal roof. Twenty metres in front of them, northbound traffic accelerated as it left the town of Nanton.

Daryl rolled the wood-stocked shotgun over. The sawed-off barrel pointed at the floor. He reached with his left hand and pulled slugs from the box inside the console. Five rounds slid easily into the chamber. He took five more from the box and tucked them into the left pocket of his canvas shirt.

Robbie adjusted his navy-blue toque, checking to make sure his ponytail was hanging over the collar of his leather jacket. "You're using slugs, right?"

Daryl nodded and rolled his left hand into a fist. "They make a nice big hole." He rubbed his clean-shaven cheeks with his right hand and inhaled the scent of gun oil. Then he reached into the glove box. A pair of black deerskin gloves lay under the 9-mm Glock. He pulled it out, ejected the magazine, checked it was full, then slid it back in. He pulled on the gloves. They fit tight along the fingers to keep them warm when he opened the window and poked the gun into the winter wind.

Robbie looked at the clock on the dash. "We should see them pretty soon. It's a gold RV with Nevada plates." He pulled a piece of paper from his jacket pocket. "Here's the number."

✕

Arthur waited at the stop sign, then pulled into the north-bound lane of the four-lane divided highway. "We'll be home just after dark." He looked west at the mountains and the sun settling onto the peaks.

Lane checked his mirror and leaned forward to take a look out Arthur's mirror. Then he turned on the camera mounted at the back of the RV. He lifted his cup from the console and savoured the last drops. "Let me know if you spot anything unusual."

✕

Daryl pointed at a gold RV with *American Revolution* painted on its side. "That them?"

Robbie checked the back seat and the AK waiting there. "You bring binoculars?"

"Nope."

Robbie shifted into drive. The tires spun on the gravel, rattling against the belly of the Suburban. He checked right, stopped at the sign, turned north on the highway, then pressed his right foot to the floor.

✕

Lane kept his eyes moving from the side mirror on the pas-senger side to the camera to the traffic ahead.

Arthur accelerated to one twenty. "Any sign of Nigel or the RCMP?"

"Not yet. Maybe we were wrong about the staff at Red's." Lane looked west at the Rocky Mountains. The sky shone orange and pink as the sun dipped down behind the peaks. "That never gets old."

"Hang on. Why is this guy so close?" Arthur jerked his thumb back in the direction of Nanton.

Lane looked in the mirror, seeing nothing. Then he looked at the rear camera. He saw a large black SUV with a

Chevrolet logo on the grill. Two men sat in the front. Lane said, "Looks like the passenger is reading a piece of paper."

"Just keep talking. Let me know what they're up to."

"They're dropping back. Soon they'll be moving into the passing lane."

"Mounties?"

Lane shook his head as he released his seat belt so he could see both mirrors and the camera. "I don't think so."

"What are you doing?" Arthur kept one eye on his side mirror and the other on the road. It ran up to the crest of a hill. "There's not much traffic out here." He spotted a white pickup truck waiting at a stop sign about five hundred metres ahead. On the other side of the highway, an SUV approached from about a kilometre away.

Arthur's the best driver. "You watch the road. I'll let you know what they're up to."

Lane crouched next to Arthur, checking the camera and then turning to look out the side window. He saw the black Chev accelerate and disappear from camera view. He looked out Arthur's side window. The passenger-side window of the Chev slid down, and the barrel of a gun appeared. "Gun!" Arthur saw the gun barrel from his side mirror and hit the air brakes. Lane was thrown against the dash, then to the floor. The Chev shot ahead. There was a puff of smoke and a pop from the shotgun. The round missed.

Lane got on his knees, left hand holding the back of the driver's chair as Arthur swung into the passing lane.

The passenger in the Chev swung the barrel around and fired again. The second round went wide.

There was a thump as Arthur's right foot slammed the accelerator to the floor. The Chev swung onto the highway's left shoulder. Arthur followed. The Chev slowed.

Arthur swung right and thumped the right rear corner of the Chev's bumper with the RV's front left bumper. The

Chev swapped ends. There was a blizzard of snow as the rear of the SUV hit the median and disappeared into the white.

Lane got to his feet. "Nice driving!"

Arthur began to slow. "We'd better stop."

"Let me take a look first." Lane stood up and rubbed the shoulder he'd bruised during Arthur's manoeuvres. "If they can get out of the Chev, we'll want to put some distance between us." He walked down the length of the RV and looked out the back window. The white pickup pulled up alongside the black Chev. The approaching blue SUV stopped on the other side. Armed officers got out of the unmarked trucks and took cover on the far side of their vehicles. "Pull over onto the shoulder and stop. Looks like we were being covered all along."

Arthur pulled over, stopped and put on the four-way flashers. They both watched from the rear window as the officers held their positions and the men inside the Chev stayed there. Five minutes later a slate-blue armoured Gurkha arrived in the southbound lane. It stopped behind the SUV.

"What's that thing?" Arthur asked.

"The intimidation factor, I think."

The pair in the Chev put their hands out the windows. Officers approached the black Chev from either side of the median. They dragged the suspects out the windows, onto the snow and then onto the pavement.

A white RCMP cruiser pulled up alongside the RV and stopped next to the driver's window. Lane walked up the passageway and opened the driver's window. Arthur stood behind him.

A female officer in the cruiser leaned to the passenger side and looked up. "You two all right?"

Lane said, "Just fine, thanks."

The officer said, "Follow me into Calgary. That pair —" she jerked her thumb in the direction of the Chev stuck in the snow "— will be transported for questioning." She pulled ahead. Arthur climbed into the driver's seat, waited for Lane to sit and put his seat belt on, then trailed their escort into Calgary. "What do we tell Cam?" Arthur asked.

"He'll know the whole story by the time we get there."

It took an hour to reach the RV dealership and drop off *American Revolution.* An unmarked grey Dodge Charger was waiting for them. The male uniformed driver, with high and tight hair, said nothing as he drove downtown and dropped them off in front of the police service office. Lane got out and zipped up his jacket. The north wind knifed through the opening at his throat. He looked over his shoulder behind the Charger and saw the driver of the RCMP cruiser pull up behind. The driver waited and watched Lane and Arthur go into the building. Another uniform — female and as uncommunicative as the driver — escorted them up the elevator and waited until they walked past Jean, who raised her eyebrows and gave a brief smile. "Welcome home."

Cam Harper sat behind his desk. He wore his navy-blue tie and shirt with its epaulets. He stood, came around the desk and shook their hands with his familiar bear-like grip. "Glad you got back safe. I hear a couple of Angels tried to mess up your trip." He motioned with his hand that they should sit.

Arthur remained standing. "Are our kids okay?"

Cam nodded. "They're fine."

Arthur sat.

Lane sat and looked out the window. *Take a good look: this will probably be the last time you see this view.* Some horizontal snowflakes blew across the glass.

Cam sat down. "Want some coffee?"

Lane nodded and reached for a cup. He could see Arthur glancing at him, then back at Harper.

Cam said, "Ottawa, Mexico City, Edmonton and Washington have been calling." He put his hands on the arms of his chair. "They want to know how much money there was and what happened to it."

Arthur held his hands up. "Not about the people who died?" He took a breath and saw Cam exhale and nod. "A bit more than three point five billion went to schools and communities on either side of the Sea of Cortez."

Harper rolled his eyes. "How exactly?"

Arthur lifted his shoulders. "We worked with some locals who divided up the money from Bonner's various accounts, then set up what are essentially trust funds to provide schools and communities with steady and reliable incomes for the next fifty years."

"What happens after fifty years?"

"That depends. If the investments do well, the money will continue." Arthur emphasized with his hands. "If not, the communities will have had fifty years to establish local economies with trained people to support them."

"You know that I have to ask you this." Harper waited for Lane or Arthur to respond. When they didn't he asked, "What did you two get out of it?"

"T-shirts," Lane said.

"What?" Harper looked at Arthur.

Lane unbuttoned his shirt to reveal a blue T-shirt with *La Luna Cortez San José* in white across the front. "They gave one to me and one to Arthur."

Cam rolled his eyes. "You two had your hands on three point five billion dollars and you got a couple of T-shirts?"

Lane shrugged. "Technically we did have the account numbers to ourselves for maybe an hour. We accepted the T-shirts as a symbolic gesture." He smiled.

Cam leaned his head to one side. "Who exactly were you working with? Alejandro?"

Arthur scratched his forehead. "And some other people."

Lane stood up. "We had a window of opportunity. We found out where Bonner kept his money. The banks and account numbers were on the labels of wine bottles from his hacienda. We took the bottles, got together with some people with particular skill sets, then drained the accounts before Pike or any of the narcos could interfere. We put the money into San José and Culiacán." He pointed at Arthur. "The idea was to put the money into those communities so there would be other economic opportunities for the locals. If we'd waited, the money would have been gone. This way, the money may do some good. Besides, the locals didn't want the narcos in San José. After Bonner and Fuentes killed a whale calf and Santa was shot, the locals wanted nothing to do with the narcos."

"What? Who killed Santa?" Cam asked.

Lane looked out the window. "A couple of Angels who thought they were killing me."

Arthur leaned back in his chair and stretched his arms. "Like the guys who tried to shoot us an hour or so ago."

Cam looked at Lane. "I've heard there was some pretty fancy driving."

Lane pointed at Arthur. "That was all him. He's the best driver."

Arthur leaned forward, then groaned when he hit vertical. "Does this mean there's no one else after us?"

Cam looked at Arthur, then at Lane. "Nope, that's not what it means, unfortunately. It looks like Pike is headed back here and he's offering a substantial paycheque for you, Lane."

X

Frederick sat in front of the computer; he wore checked pajama pants, a T-shirt and sandals. His bedroom door was shut. From upstairs came the muffled sound of his parents' favourite reality show, about some family living out in the country who hunted, preached and always had Sunday dinner together. He'd never seen a whiter family. They seldom had any contact with other people, let alone people from another culture, but talked as if they had all the answers.

Frederick plugged in his noise-cancelling headphones and put them on. He listened to some Elvis and Bowie while checking the major news pages. The story about the pair arrested south of the city caught his attention. There were few details beyond the two men being in custody.

He checked his phony email account. There was a new message from 11404.

> *Update on the Lane contract. Two hundred large provided the job is completed and I am witness to it. Most recent intel is that Lane is back in his hometown.*

chapter 22

Lane and Arthur sat in the kitchen. Arthur sipped a London Fog and Lane finished his first latté. Indiana wore one-piece dinosaur sleepers and sat in his booster chair eating grapes and raspberries. Lane looked through the opening in the kitchen wall and into the dining room, which was stacked with furniture and cardboard boxes.

"It's a little cozier than when we left," Arthur observed.

Lane got up, put a gentle hand on Indiana's cheek and walked over to the espresso machine. He turned it on, then ground some beans and locked the portafilter into place. He turned to look out the window. An unmarked unit rolled past. Then a man walking a large German shepherd–border collie cross made a point of not noticing Lane and Arthur's house. "I need to go in to work."

"I thought you were going to retire." Arthur cut a grape in half for Indiana.

Lane poured milk into a stainless-steel pitcher, put it under the spout and turned on the steam. "I need to talk with Nigel and Lori."

"I'll call Tommy while you're out." Arthur lifted Indiana then set him on his knee. "He needs to know about our legal complications."

Lane nodded as he watched the milk and listened for the rumbling grumble telling him it had reached the right temperature. He looked out the window and across the street. The recently rented neighbouring bungalow was occupied with twenty-four-hour Calgary Police Service protection.

Lane parked at the CPS office in northeast Calgary. It was in a white two-storey building connected to a fire hall. To the north and across the street, a shopping mall sprawled. A leisure centre buzzed with activity on the east side.

He looked at the sliding glass doors of the district office. *Things change so quickly. You used to be part of all of this. Soon you'll be on the outside.*

He walked inside. A thirty-something uniformed officer with a puffy white face and bulbous nose asked, "Can I help you?"

Lane recognized condescension behind the British accent and read his nametag. Daniels. "Lori is expecting me."

The officer picked up a phone. "Have a seat and I'll give her a ring." He turned his back on Lane, who sat down on an aluminum-framed chair. He looked beyond the counter and the glass. A door opened behind Daniels. Lori appeared with an eye-popping flash of red jacket. Lane knew the rest of her outfit would be coordinated with that exact shade.

Lori pointed at Daniels. "George! Why the hell are you making him wait? He's one of our homicide detectives."

Daniels reddened and puffed himself up. "He didn't identify himself!"

Lane stood up and smiled at his friend. She opened the door next to the counter. She wore red leggings and boots to match the mid-thigh-length jacket. "So you did get a tan! Come on, I'll show you the new digs." She ignored Daniels, gave Lane a hug, then waited for Lane to hold the door for her as she led the way to a large room with a series of cubicles. At the front were three whiteboards already covered with notes, photos and papers.

Lori pointed at an office behind glass. "Your desk is there. With the restructuring, everything had to move fast. I hope I got everything from your old office. They were very careful with the computer and the oversized monitor."

"Thank you." He walked to the whiteboards and began to absorb information. He noticed the picture of a young man next to the faces of four older men. He recognized one of the four from Mexico and another from yesterday on the highway. "What's this group all about?"

"They are all suspected of taking contracts on your life." Lori crossed her arms and leaned her rear up against a desk.

Lane looked around the room. "Is Nigel here?"

She nodded in the direction of a windowless metal door. "They're in the conference room."

"Things have changed."

"They have. Your investigation got bigger than expected. Harper and the mayor are worried about a gang war. Welcome to a new way of doing things. Want me to introduce you?" She turned her head to one side and lifted her eyebrows.

Play along. "If you like."

She leaned close. "You're a big boy. Just knock." She turned and headed for her desk.

Lane took another look around the room at the cubicles, the whiteboards, the tinted windows and the grey carpet. He walked up to the door, knocked, then eased it open.

Four people were sitting at a square table. Lane recognized two. Nigel looked at a screen as he typed information into his laptop. Malik Wajdan sat nearby. He was just over six feet tall and had dark hair, brown eyes and an angular face. He was the first member of his family to be born in Canada. Lane had been there when he was interviewed for a position in homicide.

Nigel said, "This is our person of interest in two separate gang-related shootings. He has no record and is — I'm not making this up — presently in grade twelve."

Lane watched as a photograph appeared on the screen. The boy had a round face and hair straight out of an Elvis movie. "His name is Frederick Lee," Nigel said.

The guy at the table with the strong chin wore a navy-blue jacket and pants. "This is the one planning on cashing Lane's contract?"

Nigel sat up in his chair. "We have recorded confirmation. Pike has offered two hundred thousand."

"What do we need to get Lee off the street?" Malik asked.

Nigel tapped the keys of his laptop. "Blood evidence was found in the Mustang used in the Stoney Trail killings. We need to get DNA evidence from Lee to begin with."

Lane inhaled. "Do you want me to ask him for a sample? I really don't like being a target or having people like Pike and his Angels taking potshots at my family."

The guy with the lantern jaw appeared unaffected by Lane's arrival. "You know, that might be the way to go. Lee thinks he's under the radar. Having Lane confront him would change the psychology of the situation. Lee is a predator and not accustomed to being hunted."

A woman sitting next to Lantern Jaw said, "You know, Dave, Lee handled himself pretty well against those two guys on Stoney Trail. They're dead. Lee's alive." The woman appeared to be in her early thirties; she had blonde hair and an angelic face. The face and the blunt honesty of the voice were incongruous. *She sounds like a truck driver when she opens her mouth.*

"As long as we think this through and kill the snake instead of scorching it," Malik said.

Trucker Voice snapped, "Will you quit quoting fucking Shakespeare?"

Nigel stood up. "Maybe we should do some introductions." He walked around the table. "This is Paul Lane." He pointed at Trucker Voice. "Angela Olsen. You know

Malik Wajdan and this is Dave Sugar." The three nodded a greeting.

Dave leaned forward. "Where's the money?"

Get to the point. I like it. "Invested in the communities of San José and Culiacán."

Angela pointed a finger. "What about handling fees?"

Lane shrugged and shook his head. "We came home with our suitcases." He held his hands out palms up. "Got a ride to San Diego, then a motorhome delivery to Calgary. There's this network of people who are trying to make things better in Mexico. Up until a week ago I didn't know it existed. All the money we recovered — three point five billion dollars — went into the communities." He lifted his hands. "Mexico's reputation for corruption to the contrary, no palms were greased."

Malik pulled out the empty chair next to him. "Want to sit down?"

Lane looked at Angela, then at Dave. "Sit down," Angela said.

Dave looked at her. "Maybe he would like a cup of coffee?"

Angela's blue eyes turned glacial. "If you want a fucking cup of coffee, you can get your own!"

Laughter blasted the room. Angela smiled, took off her right shoe and waved it at Dave. When the laughter died, she looked at Lane. "I guess you know Pike is offering Lee extra if he gets to watch your execution."

Nigel tapped the table with a pen. "We have a plan we'd like to run past you."

✕

Lane sat in his new office. The windows looked out across the tops of a grey cubicle maze. Tinted windows allowed a limited amount of natural light to enter. He switched on his computer and adjusted the oversized screen. It took a moment for the screen to come to life.

Lane's phone rang. He reached into his jacket pocket, read the incoming number and tapped the face of his smartphone. "What's up?"

Arthur chewed on some kind of nut. "Tommy Pham called."

"And?"

"He wants to meet with us this afternoon at three. He says it's very important to get out in front of something like this, get the truth out and let people know what really happened. Otherwise he thinks we'll be on the defensive when the accusations come."

"He's got a plan?"

"Yes. A Melissa Ng will be contacting you."

Lane tapped the mouse with his free hand, put the phone on speaker, set it down and entered his computer password. "Who's she?"

"Part of Uncle Tran's family. She works for the CBC."

"I don't much like reporters." He leaned back in his chair and opened his mapping program. *I can start filling in names and details, then take a look at the big picture.*

"Tommy recommends her. Says she's tough and fair."

Lane sat next to Arthur in Tommy Pham's conference room. The windows looked across the river into Chinatown with office towers in the background and the Rocky Mountains peeking out around the edges.

Tommy Pham wore a white shirt, a red tie and about twenty more pounds than the last time they had met. His hair was still black, his eyes revealed an intelligence coming from the far right of the bell curve and he moved like a dancer in brogues. He shook hands with Lane and Arthur, then sat down across from them. He looked at his watch. "She is on her way."

Arthur looked at Lane. "Melissa Ng is going to be here. I forgot to tell you."

Lane looked at Tommy, who was watching him. "She is your cousin?"

Tommy nodded.

The door opened and in stepped a round-faced woman with short black hair. She wore a red blouse, black knee-high boots and black yoga pants. She closed the door. It rattled back and forth against the lock. She smiled, took in the room and pointed at Lane. "You're the detective and you are Arthur." Melissa gave them both firm handshakes and sat down at the head of the table with Arthur on her right and Tommy on her left. She pulled an iPad from her red leather purse and set it on the table. Then she rolled out a keyboard. Melissa tapped the face. "Where's the money?"

Arthur asked, "If we tell you, what will you do to protect the schools and communities from having the money taken away from them?"

Melissa studied them. "Explain."

Arthur closed his mouth. Lane looked at Tommy, who nodded. The detective turned his eyes back to Melissa. "We found cartel account numbers and banks. We worked with some people who were able to transfer the funds from Bonner's cartel accounts into—" He looked at Arthur.

Arthur looked out the window. "A kind of trust fund. The money will gather interest while communities and schools are provided with extra money every month for their budgets."

"How much?" Melissa tapped the keypad.

Lane said, "Three point five."

"Million?"

"Billion," Arthur said.

Melissa glanced at Tommy, who lifted his eyebrows. She looked at Arthur. "How much did you keep for expenses?"

She sounds skeptical.

Arthur turned to face her. "None. All of it went into the communities so that they can support and build local economies separate from the drug trade. Now, what can you do to make sure the various governments and the narcos won't be able to take the money back from the communities?"

Tommy interlocked his fingers and waited for Melissa to reply.

She frowned. "There are no guarantees." She looked at her keyboard then at Tommy. "I need to verify your story before getting the word out. And that's assuming Mr. Bonner's cartel money actually ended up where you say it did."

Keep your mouth shut and let her do the talking. Lane scratched the tip of his nose, then gave a gentle shake of the head to Arthur. *I hope he understands.*

Arthur took a deep breath. "You can assume what you like. You can assume a couple of Angels tried to kill us on the highway just north of Nanton. You can also assume that if we give you the names of people who helped get the money to the communities in Mexico—and these are by no means wealthy people—that their lives will be in danger as well."

I guess he didn't get the hint.

Melissa sat back and studied Arthur for a minute. "So it is true. A couple of Hells Angels tried to carry out a contract on you." She pointed at Lane.

He looked at her, shrugged, then looked at his partner. "Arthur took care of them."

Arthur shook his head. "We worked together."

Melissa pointed a finger at Arthur. "So you won't give me specifics. What else can you tell me?"

Lane shook his head. "Not much. If we give you much more, we put people's lives at risk. The Angels shot Santa outside the resort we were staying at because they were looking for a guy with a beard."

Tommy covered his mouth but his eyes gave him away.

Melissa laughed. "You're joking!"

Arthur frowned. "It happened in front of us."

"That and a pair of whales took care of Bonner, Manny and Fuentes." Lane pulled out his phone to check the time.

Melissa sat back open mouthed. "What exactly do you mean by 'taking care of Bonner, Manny and Fuentes'?"

Arthur rolled his eyes. "The whales killed them after they shot and killed their calf. The calf washed up on the beach in front of our resort. The mother and nurse tracked a cigarette boat, swamped it, then swatted the men in the water."

Melissa put her index finger on the table. "This is unbelievable." She looked at Tommy. "Do you believe any of this?"

Tommy turned to her. "If it was anyone else, I would have to say no. Lane has never lied to me before, so I think the story at least deserves verification."

Melissa studied Lane, who looked back at her to see if she had more questions. Instead she tucked her iPad in her bag, stood and walked out the door.

✕

Frederick sat in his Mercedes waiting for Brittany. He was parked in the lot behind his school. The sun was shining but the temperature was close to freezing. He reached over and turned on the heated seat. Then he tapped the face of his smartphone to check for messages. The first was from Pike. *In town this week. When and where is the job scheduled?*

There was a tap on the glass next to his face. Frederick looked right and into the face of a blue-eyed man with mostly grey hair and one missing earlobe. He wore a grey coat with the collar turned up. Frederick was frozen for a moment when he realized where he'd seen the face before.

The man tapped again. His face was a blank mask.

Frederick reached for the switch and the window hummed open.

"Frederick Lee?"

Frederick nodded. "What do you want?"

"I'm Detective Lane of the Calgary Police Service." He nodded, lifting his chin to indicate that Frederick should look to his left. "This is Detective Li."

Frederick looked at the freckle-faced man on the passenger side. Li had wild black hair. Lee turned back to Lane. "Okay."

"We'd like to ask you some questions," Lane said.

Frederick smiled. "Of course." He opened the passenger window.

Nigel leaned inside. "We were wondering if you could check the calendar on your phone and see where you were the night of November fourth?"

Lane tapped the leather on Frederick's headrest. "While you're at it, would you check the night of November sixth as well? We're specifically interested in your whereabouts after nine p.m."

Frederick tapped the face of his phone and opened his calendar. "I think that I was home both nights. My parents will vouch for me."

Nigel pulled out his phone and tapped the face. "I'd like their contact information."

Frederick smiled. "Sure. No problem. Ready?"

Nigel nodded.

Frederick rattled off the home, cell and work numbers of his parents. "Anything else?"

Lane tapped Frederick on the shoulder, noticed that the boy winced and smiled back. "No, that's great. We thought you should meet us face to face. See you soon." He turned and walked back to the unmarked Ford.

A moment later, Nigel climbed in behind the wheel.

Lane said, "That takes care of that part of your plan."

"Now we wait for Rendon to tell us who Frederick contacts." He started the car, backed up and drove out of the parking lot.

×

Alex Rendon stood and watched his three main computer screens while eating a bowl of what his father liked to call meatball soup. Dad made the meatballs and tomato sauce from scratch. This time the sauce had celery and red, orange and yellow peppers added. Alex used the edge of his spoon to break a meatball in half. Then he blew on the meat until he could pop the still dangerously hot morsel into his mouth.

He chewed while Frederick Lee's text message began to walk its way onto the screen. *Cops are asking questions. You need to sweeten the deal. Lane was waiting for me after school.*

"Definitely a good sign," Alex said.

Pike's reply came about a minute later. *Get a burner.*

Alex picked up his cell phone.

chapter 23

Funding Local Economies Aimed at Undermining Cartels

Redistribution defended as a new approach to ending the drug war

CBC NEWS POSTED NOV. 25, 5:16 A.M. MT

An estimated $3.5 billion of drug cartel money with connections to Canada has been seized and redistributed to communities in Mexico. Drug profits have been diverted to support schools and hospitals on either side of the Sea of Cortez.

Arthur Merali, a Calgary accountant, played an integral role in the reallocation of these funds. He and his partner, Paul Lane, a member of the Calgary Police Service, were on vacation in San José, Mexico, when locals approached them.

"They needed help fighting back against the violence and intimidation that is brought about by international drug trafficking, and the inability of local officials to end the war on drugs," says Merali.

The identities of those in Mexico responsible for the redirection of these assets are being protected to ensure their safety. The connection to Canada is part of an ongoing drug investigation.

The Mexican communities involved include San José del Cabo, Cabo San Lucas and Culiacán.

Continue reading

Lane rolled over onto his hands and knees. He took a deep breath, then peered overtop of his desk. Lori stood above him, her hands leaning on the other side of the desk. The light from the windows lit one side of her blonde hair, and her white blouse made her appear angelic. "What the fuck are you doing here? Arthur called me at home wondering where you are and if you're okay. I came to work an hour early to find you sleeping."

"I was working late." His mouth tasted like dusty carpet.

Lori rolled her eyes. "Don't give me that. You're hiding out. Not going home because that kid and Pike are trying to kill you. You don't want to be around Arthur or the kids in case they become collateral damage."

Lane tried to hide the blush on his face as he got to his feet. *Lori, you're just smarter than the average momma bear.*

"Just tell me the truth. How close are you to nailing these guys?" She stood with her back to the door and her arms crossed.

He looked on his desk and spotted two cups of coffee stuck in a paper tray. His eyes met Lori's.

"Don't get used to it." She pulled one of the cups from the tray and handed it to him; the other cup took a little more encouragement. "Well? How close are you? I'm not going to babysit you all week, you know."

He took a sip of coffee. *Mocaccino!* "Twenty-four to thirty-six hours. Pike is either here or very close. He and Lee are going to work out the details."

Lori pointed a clear-coated nail at him. "Alex Rendon is listening in?"

"That's right."

"Let's get this mess cleaned up so you can go home." She turned and opened the door. "After you have a shower, you're taking me for breakfast."

Forty-five minutes later they were sitting in a booth next to a window. Lane sat so he could see the front door, the washrooms and the entrance to the kitchen.

Lori sipped her tea. "Aren't you going to eat your omelette?"

He looked at the omelette oozing cheddar cheese, the four slices of whole grain toast and the wedge of orange. *I really should eat.* He picked up his fork, sliced off the end of the omelette and put it in his mouth. It tasted like paste but he chewed mechanically and swallowed anyway. All the while his eyes scanned the incoming and outgoing patrons and the outside traffic.

Lori set her cup down. "I know about Nigel's plan but I need to know what your plan is."

Okay. "Stay away from my family until this is over. Deal with Lee and Pike then decide."

"Decide?"

"What to do next."

Lori looked up from her fruit cup. "You're done, then?"

Lane put another fork full of omelette in his mouth. "I want to spend some time watching Indiana growing up."

Lori winked. "And what will you do in your spare time?"

The man who walked into Lane's office wore a navy-blue sports jacket, white shirt and black tie. His face was shaved to shiny and his blond hair had a precise high-and-tight cut. He stuck out his hand. "Robert Whitemore. I'm with internal investigations."

Lane set his third cup of coffee on the desk and shook. He felt his mind running laps and his mouth did the same. "You're a Lost Boy."

Whitemore took a moment to study Lane. "Your niece was at Paradise."

Lane waited. *I've been expecting you and it looks like you've done your homework.*

Whitemore took a phone from his jacket pocket. "Mind if I record our conversation?"

"Go ahead." Lane reached for his coffee and held it with both hands.

Whitemore closed the door, sitting down next to Lane in a chair by the wall. He fiddled with his phone, then set it on the nearest corner of the desk. "I am in Detective Paul Lane's office. He has agreed to allow the recording of this conversation."

"That is correct. You haven't answered my question." Lane sipped his coffee.

Whitemore nodded. "Yes. I was excommunicated from Paradise when I was fifteen and I am what you might call a Lost Boy."

Lane waited.

"What was the amount of your compensation from the three point five billion dollars recovered from Luis Bonner's estate in Palmilla, Mexico?"

"A T-shirt."

Whitemore lifted his chin, took a slow breath, then exhaled. "I'm referring to monetary compensation. In other words, what was your share of the take?"

"Zero."

"What was Arthur Merali's share of the take?"

"Zero."

Whitemore's grey eyes studied Lane. "What other forms of compensation did you receive?"

"A contract was taken out on my life. Arthur and I were ambushed on the highway just north of Nanton. At this moment, Sean Pike has offered two hundred thousand dollars for my life."

"Yes. Two men are already in custody."

"Two Angels."

Whitemore looked at his hands. "You are referring to members of the Hells Angels Motorcycle Club?"

"Yes. A member of the Angels, Manny Posadowski, was observed in several meetings with Luis Bonner, Ignacio Enrique and Sean Pike in Mexico earlier this month."

"You are referring to Manny Posadowski of the Calgary chapter of the Hells Angels?"

Lane nodded as he adjusted the cardboard heat jacket on his cup. "We had a choice. Either leave the wine bottles with the account numbers or take them and transfer the money into communities where it might do some good."

"Wine bottles?"

"Bonner printed the account numbers and respective bank names on wine labels. We observed Fuentes and Posadowski leaving an art gallery with bottles of wine. When we searched Bonner's Palmilla estate, the connection was made. We were able to leave the estate with the bottles, set up new accounts and transfer the money to the San José and Culiacán accounts before any cartel members could access the funds."

"Chief Harper is under pressure because Ottawa, Washington and Mexico City want to know what happened to the money."

Lane shrugged. "And Pike wants me dead."

"Rendon is monitoring Pike and Lee. This ends our session." Whitemore reached over and shut off the recording.

"I'm tired of having my family mixed up in messes like this. The Angels would have killed Arthur if he wasn't lucky." Lane inhaled. "And a good driver."

Robert picked up his phone and slid it into his inside jacket pocket. "That's why you're not worried about this internal investigation?"

Lane shook his head. "I can only tell you the truth about

the cartel's money. My family is the priority right now. I have to draw Lee and Pike out and away from my family."

"You took in a niece and nephew, didn't you?"

"Arthur and I did."

"An aunt took me in. She was excommunicated from the church and she took me in. I was lucky." Whitemore stared at a spot in the distance just above and behind Lane's head.

"So maybe you understand," Lane said.

Whitemore stood up. "Maybe I do. But I still have to do my job."

"Understood." Lane lifted his cup of coffee and tried to smile.

"I'll be in touch." Whitemore left.

Lane went back to work on the map he'd created on the metre-wide monitor. He put the pieces for Mexico on one side and was filling in names and events from Calgary on the other.

There was a knock on the glass. He looked up and saw Arthur, who opened the door, stepped inside and closed the door behind him. "What's going on?"

"It's busy." *That sounds so lame.*

Arthur waved the excuse away with the swipe of a hand. "You're hiding out to keep them away from us."

Lane shrugged, saving the data he'd added to his map.

Arthur came around the desk and looked at the screen. "Move over. I want to take a look."

Lane got up and sat down in a chair next to the desk.

There was a knock and the door opened. Nigel was staring at the face of his phone. "We've had some problems with the 911 centre. Rendon has been keeping an eye on a few of Pike's old friends. One of those officers got a call from a burner phone. Rendon recognized the caller. It was Pike. He traced Pike's next call. It was to Frederick Lee. You're going to get a call from the 911 centre tonight. It'll be a —"

Nigel spotted Arthur when Lane's partner leaned around the edge of the monitor.

"Where will it happen?" Arthur asked.

Nigel looked at Lane, who shrugged. "Well?"

Nigel puffed out his cheeks as he exhaled. "We've got some planning to do. McTavish still doing tactical?"

Lane looked out the glass and saw Lori approaching. "No, it's some new guy. McTavish retired."

Lori stepped inside the office. She nodded at Arthur. "Rendon, Harper and Singh, the new tactical leader, are on their way. The Chief wants to meet in the conference room in twenty-five minutes."

✕

Frederick parked his Mercedes in the garage. The door clunked shut and the overhead light came on. He looked at the green digital clock, noting it was twelve noon: ten hours before his parents would be home.

He climbed down from the SUV, then walked to the furthest corner of the garage, opposite from the door into the house. A padlocked red metal toolbox sat on the floor underneath a couple of empty cardboard boxes. He pushed the boxes to one side, then used a key to open the toolbox padlock. He lifted the lid. From the top shelf, he took three twenty-round clips. He lifted the shelf and pulled out a plastic-wrapped Kevlar vest. Underneath the vest was a polished metal case. He lifted it out, opened it and grabbed the Steyr tactical machine pistol and a couple of thirty-round magazines. He closed and locked the toolbox, then set the Steyr and the vest on the floor behind the passenger seat in the Mercedes. A new Beretta was in the glove compartment. He reached inside, set the handgun and magazines on the seat, reached for a box of shells and began to load rounds into magazines.

His burner chirped. He set the half-full magazine down, pulled the phone from his jacket pocket and read a text from Brittany. *WHERE ARE YOU?* He put the phone down, picked up the magazine and finished loading.

He slid the full magazine into the pocket of his jacket, then picked up his phone and tapped a text. *Got a promotion. Go home after school. Get your passport. We need to be in Edmonton by 6 a.m. tomorrow to catch a flight to Cabo.*

He pressed send and went back to loading magazines.

×

Alex Rendon took a bite from a double burger. He covered his mouth with his left hand. "The short of it is that Pike and Lee plan to lure you into a trap tonight." He closed his mouth and pointed at Lane. "And kill you." They sat with Nigel, Harper and Harvinder Singh around the conference table.

Singh wore her grey–blue tactical unit uniform with a Glock strapped to her right hip. Her brown hair was tied back and her brown eyes focused on Lane. "We will have units on standby at all four quadrants of the city. I will take the northwest." She pointed at Lane. "I want you to be in constant communication with me. Alex will fix you up."

Harper sat next to Lane. Harper wore navy-blue pants, shirt and tie. "I want Nigel to be in communication as well as a backup. I want built-in redundancies and no mistakes when we take Lee and Pike down. Pike is especially dangerous because he knows our tactics and protocols."

Singh nodded. "Each of the other three teams will head for the indicated location once the dispatcher makes the call to Lane. HAWCS will be airborne as soon as the call is received."

"Lacey?" Lane asked.

Singh smiled. "That's right."

Nigel turned to Lane. "She the one who flew with you when Jones was driving his pickup with the nitro?"

Lane nodded. "I ride alone on this one."

Nigel hit the table with an open palm. "What?"

Lane looked at his partner. "I know you'll have my back. That's not the issue. I will be alone in the vehicle." He looked around the table. "I trust that each of you will do your respective jobs. And I trust you will allow me to do mine."

Harper turned to look sideways at Lane. "What is the issue, then?"

Lane leaned his elbows on the table and pointed at Rendon. "Your information indicates that Pike will be there. There will be at least two shooters. I want all of the tactical officers on the periphery because that's where Pike will be. Lee is covered. I want you —" he pointed at Nigel "— out there to make sure Pike is covered as well."

Nigel nodded.

Harper looked at Singh. "Does that work for you?"

She nodded. "It does. My team will have Lane covered. We could use an extra pair of eyes watching for any other threats."

Harper looked at each team member in turn. "Let's get the job done."

The call came a little after seven that night. Lane was leaving the washroom when his phone rang. Nigel stood about nine metres away. He watched and listened as Lane answered. "Lane."

"Dispatch here. We have a caller who claims to have information on the Sleeping Dragon shootings. Should I connect your call?"

"Go ahead." Lane heard voices echoing in the background before the person spoke.

"If you want to find out what happened at the Sleeping Dragon, meet me in twenty minutes. I will be under the number 6 North light pole next to the Market Mall recycling depot. It's at the northeast corner of the mall parking lot." Frederick pressed end on his burner phone, dropped it in a garbage can and kept walking north past Twisted Goods at the south end of the mall. He hefted a black backpack with the weight of four magazines, a Beretta and the Steyr. He adjusted the right strap of the backpack, feeling for the Kevlar vest under his navy-blue hoodie.

×

Arthur watched Lane put on his ceramic body armour and walk across the office followed by Nigel. Arthur got up from behind the desk and walked to Lori's cubicle. She was watching Lane and Nigel as they stepped up to the door then outside. "Where are they going?" Arthur asked.

She turned to him. "Where you can't go."

He shook his head. "Watch me." He turned and walked away.

Lori ran after him. "You're going to need this." Arthur found he couldn't articulate a reply as she handed him a black walkie-talkie. "It's set to their frequency."

He took the radio, kissed her on the cheek, then walked to the door. Outside, he reached into his pocket, opened the door to their black BMW X3, climbed in and set the radio on the passenger seat.

×

Lane took Stoney Trail and drove west toward the mountains. The streetlights attempted to push back the November darkness. The days would continue to get shorter for another few weeks. He passed a semi and the cabin of the Chev filled with the hum of eighteen wheels. He took the exit to Shaganappi Trail and headed south. Traffic was light. He used the flashing blue-and-white lights on the Chev ghost car and made good time. He had five minutes to spare when he crossed overtop Crowchild Trail, turned off the lights and slowed. He turned right at 40th Avenue, looking left at the scattering of parked cars and green recycling bins lined up at the northeastern corner of the parking lot. Evergreens and grey poplars clustered behind the bins. The northernmost store in the mall was about one hundred metres away.

He turned left into the lot and took his time counting the cars parked in the northeast corner. He saw nine. He drove further south, then turned left and slowed to follow the eastern edge of the lot as he worked his way north again to the last light pole with 6 North painted in white on a yellow background.

×

Singh sat in the rear seat of a Ford pickup parked south of Lane's location. It faced north and east. The Ford had tinted windows at the sides and back. She leaned forward between the Ford's front seats. She used her Nikon binoculars to sweep the area while Lane's Chev approached the light pole. She noted the locations of each member of her team.

Her peripheral vision spotted motion to her left. A white pickup truck was towing a white contractor's trailer, two and a half metres wide and six metres long. The driver parked near the light pole, got out of the truck and walked toward the mall.

Singh's radio received a warning. "Robertson blocked. Shifting position."

She looked toward the office building one hundred metres away. She couldn't see her sharpshooter Robertson on the roof but knew he was there.

A lone figure walked toward Lane and the parked Chev. The figure wore a black backpack, hoodie, pants and shoes. His hands were tucked in the kangaroo pocket of the hoodie. Singh lifted her radio and said, "Subject approaching from the south. Approximately seventy-five metres from Lane."

Lane watched the driver of the white pickup reach around and hitch the back of his jeans. The man walked toward the mall. Then Lane spotted the man in the black hoodie approaching. Lane felt a familiar tickle of anxiety in his belly. He lifted the Glock from its holster. His left hand went for the Chev's door handle.

The figure in the hoodie pulled his left hand from the pouch. His right came out with a handgun.

Lane opened the door. His left foot touched the pavement.

The hatch of a dark-coloured SUV swung open. An officer dressed in a grey–blue tactical team uniform levelled a C8 assault rifle at the hooded figure.

The lights of Singh's pickup coned the hooded figure in their glare. She climbed into the front seat, started the engine and shifted into drive. Lane stood, cupped the butt of the Glock in his left hand and aimed at the figure.

A tactical team pair stepped from the back of a minivan. They aimed their weapons at the figure and walked deliberately toward him.

Frederick Lee looked away from Lane and at the approaching pair.

Singh pulled the pickup to within ten metres of Lee. She opened the door. "Down on your knees!"

Lee hesitated as he looked back at Lane.

Nigel walked along the edge of the lot to the south of Lane. He spotted a familiar black BMW turning into the lot and reached for his radio.

Singh's radio said, "The black BMW is a friendly." Her eyes were glued to Lee, who had dropped to his knees. "Face down on the pavement!"

Lane heard the whispering thrum of the incoming HAWCS helicopter.

Frederick lay face down. The approaching pair of officers stood over him. One kicked the gun away. The other pulled off the backpack.

Lane stepped out from behind the Chev's open door. A bullet hit between his shoulder blades. He took a step forward. A second bullet smacked the ribs on his right side. A third hit him just below the ceramic vest. He tried to inhale and discovered he couldn't. His left hand reached out as he fell forward. The Glock smacked the pavement and broke his right thumb. His mind focused as he struggled to understand what was happening.

Lane rolled onto his back. He began a mental checklist of his body. He could feel his toes. He rolled his ankles. His left hand moved to the lower right quadrant of his abdomen. He brought the hand close to his nose and could smell blood. He looked up at the four lights atop a pole illuminating this corner of the mall's parking lot.

Above that he saw the spotlight slung under the belly of the HAWCS helicopter. *Lacey will be here soon.*

There were footsteps and Lane rolled his head to the left. A tactical officer approached from the east. He held a handgun and wore a helmet, yellow glasses and a grey–blue uniform under a Kevlar vest. *Why does he have a silencer?*

Lane took a shallow breath. The pain was sharp and immediate.

The helmeted officer stood a few metres away. He looked down and aimed at Lane's forehead.

It's Pike! Lane tried to lift his Glock but the broken thumb made it impossible.

Pike exhaled a cloud of breath. Lane saw every detail of his face. The eyes behind the yellow glasses. The round face. Chin cupped by the helmet strap. Lane saw Pike grimace. *Right, his shoulder was dislocated by the whale.*

"Stan's killer got away because of you," Pike said. "I'm going to kill her next." He smiled.

"Stop!" Nigel yelled. There was a gunshot.

Pike shuddered.

Another gunshot.

Lane focused on Pike's trigger finger. He heard the sound of an engine. Pike looked to his left. He was illuminated by headlights. Lane heard the solid thump of meat hitting metal, followed by a boom of metal, flesh and plastic pounding into one of the recycling bins. A horn blared. An engine raced and died.

Lane heard running feet on pavement. Time was a rubber band flexing and stretching. Then Nigel was there on his knees. "Are you hit?"

Pain ripped through him. Lane fought to concentrate on breathing. *Breathe in as deep as you can. Exhale slowly.*

Singh knelt on the other side of him, her eyes wide and calm. She put her hand on his belly just below the vest. She spoke to someone he could not see. "Lane's got a gunshot wound to the abdomen. We need to put him on HAWCS now!"

Arthur handed something to Singh, saying, "I always have a few of these with me." Lane recognized the object was a diaper. Singh flipped it open with her free hand, then lifted her left hand and pressed down again. She looked over her shoulder. "The suspects are disarmed?"

A voice spoke from out of Lane's range of vision. "Both immobilized." Dust swirled around him. He looked up at the lights, seeing a momentary sundog.

"Paul?"

Lane recognized the voice. "Why are you here, Arthur?"

Singh's voice was matter of fact. "He and Nigel took care of the second shooter." Lane felt her hand pressing down on the wound as he was rolled onto his side. *Breathe. Just breathe.*

"It's a through and through. Get the stretcher sling," Singh said. "Got another diaper?"

He felt pressure against his back. Someone loosened his belt, pulled it free, then used it to pull the diapers snug against the wounds in his abdomen and back. He swallowed hard to push down the nausea.

Lane felt himself being rolled from one shoulder to the other. He was lifted in a sling. He counted three officers on his right. Two more plus Singh were on his left. They walked him under the wash of the helicopter's rotors. As they hefted him up to slide him through the rear door, he got a glimpse of Pike — the helmeted head and arms of a man on the crumpled hood of Arthur's black BMW. The corpse was pinned between the SUV and a green recycling bin.

The helicopter door closed. For a moment Lane felt a kind of muted clarity before the helicopter lifted off. He saw a silhouette leaning over him. He saw the glow from the instruments. Then a widening darkness. First his peripheral vision was gone. His focus quickly narrowed to the helmet and pair of yellow lenses in front of him. *It feels like being under water. Just swim with the current.* He closed his eyes.

He heard Singh's voice. "Lane? Lane?"

chapter 24

Officer Critical, One Man Dead, One in Custody

Shooting at Market Mall signals a further escalation in the city's gang war

CBC NEWS POSTED NOV. 26, 1:16 P.M. MT

A Calgary Police officer is in critical condition at the Foothills Medical Centre after a shooting in the parking lot of Market Mall Tuesday night.

Another man was pronounced dead at the scene and a third is in custody. No names have been released pending notification of next of kin.

At a news conference Wednesday morning, Calgary Chief of Police Cameron Harper said the officer was a twenty-eight-year veteran. The shooter died at the scene. An armed accomplice arrested Tuesday night was a person of interest in another shooting earlier this month.

The northeast corner of the Market Mall parking lot remains cordoned off as evidence continues to be gathered.

This is the latest in a spate of shootings that began in early November. Sources in the Calgary Police Service attribute the violence to escalating tensions between rival gangs.

Continue reading

ACKNOWLEDGEMENTS

Thank you, Dr. Husain.

Again, thanks to Tony Bidulka and the late Wayne Gunn.

Thank you, Deanne, for the medical advice on gunshot wounds.

Jeremy, thank you for the Tactical Unit weapon information supplied at MEC.

Thanks to Richard for the Thursday-morning feedback sessions.

Thank you, David Sweet, for generously sharing your knowledge and expertise. Ben, thank you for arranging the interview.

Emir, thank you for sharing the plans for the house at Palmilla.

To all the people at NeWest Press (including Claire and Matt) who supported the novels over the years, thank you. A big thank-you to Leslie Vermeer, who came to know the characters as well as I do. Thank you, Leslie, for your precise editing. The books are so much better after you work your magic on them. Thank you Natalie of Kisscut Design for the amazing cover and interior designs.

Karma, thank you for the Spanish translations.

Thanks to creative writers at Nickle, Bowness, Lord Beaverbrook, Alternative, Forest Lawn and Queen Elizabeth.

Thank you to Stephen of Sage Innovations (garryryan.ca).

Thank you to the people who run independent bookstores like Pages Books, Shelf Life Books and Owl's Nest Books in Calgary.

Sharon, Karma, Ben, Luke, Indiana and Ella, thank you for your love and support. The novels are about family, and you are the inspiration.

In 2004, Garry Ryan published his first Detective Lane novel, *Queen's Park*. The second, *The Lucky Elephant Restaurant*, won a 2007 Lambda Literary Award. He has since published eight more titles in the series. In 2009, Ryan was awarded Calgary's Freedom of Expression Award. He currently lives in Calgary.